What Happened at Hawthorne House

What Happened at Hawthorne House

by Hadassah Shiradski

Brigids Gate
PRESS

What Happened at Hawthorne House

Copyright 2023 © Hadassah Shiradski

This book is a work of fiction. All of the characters, organizations, and events portrayed in this story are either products of the author's imagination or are used fictitiously. Any resemblance to actual events or locales or persons, living or dead, is entirely coincidental.

All rights reserved. No part of this publication may be reproduced in any form or by any means without the express written permission of the publisher, except in the case of brief excerpts in critical reviews or articles.

Edited by: Stephanie Ellis
Proofed and formatted by: Stephanie Ellis
Cover illustration and design by: Miblart

First Edition: August 2023

ISBN (paperback): 978-1-957537-62-7
ISBN (ebook): 978-1-957537-61-0
Library of Congress Control Number: 2023943018

BRIGIDS GATE PRESS

Bucyrus, Kansas

www.brigidsgatepress.com

Printed in the United States of America

For Grandma and Papa

Content warnings are provided at the end of this book

Part One – The Clover Court

(November 1926)

Prologue

We were bored, and so we made up a game. We were bored of reading the same books and playing the same games, and so we made up a new game. We were bored of pretending to get along when we didn't like living with each other, and so we made up a game of one-uppance, of besting each other in pranks and tricks. A game that we each had a chance of winning. A pretend game of a Queen and a court of Princesses. A game set in our castle, which the adults called 'Hawthorne House'.

Chapter One – Crown

The polished hardwood floorboards were cold against her legs, chilled from the draught that came in under the closed door. Raindrops pattered intermittently against the large windows, ebbing with the gusts of wind. Rosalyn sighed as she leaned against the bookcase that stood tall behind her, feeling the handsome spines press against her back and shoulders. The Clover Court was just beginning to properly form, and every detail had to be perfect.

"Give that back, it's mine!" A familiar voice snapped with the kind of petulance that was only found in people who didn't like to share even when they were told to, and Rosalyn opened her eyes, distracted from her thoughts. Turning her head just in time, she watched Marie snatch the red crayon out of Sophie's hand and push her backwards, away from the sheets of scribble-filled paper that lay haphazardly between and around the two of them.

Sophie fell back—just a bit, mind, not enough to disturb the Very Important and Necessary drawings—and composed herself with that little huff she gave whenever she was mildly annoyed or extremely angry. She lifted a hand to straighten and smooth down her dress until the indigo cloth was immaculate again, then plucked a brown crayon up from the floor and knelt down to start drawing what looked like an old-fashioned scroll—the kind that messengers used to carry between castles in wartimes of old.

"This will be the decree that ..." Sophie paused in her intonation for a moment, lifting her head to stare at Rosalyn, who was sitting to one side of the too-big living room, then apparently reconsidered the nature of what she was drawing. "Actually, it's a charter."

Although she didn't like talking to Sophie, because she was strange and rude and once locked Rosalyn in that cupboard with all the spiders for a whole afternoon, she was nicer than the only other girl around their age in this place, so Rosalyn finally spoke up.

"A charter? Whatever for?"

Sophie rolled her eyes as though Rosalyn was as stupid as Matron kept saying they all were, as if it was their fault for not having parents. "For the Royal Clover Court roster, *Rosalyn*. Weren't you listening at cleaning time?"

Rosalyn felt her teeth grit as she recalled exactly why she hadn't been there at cleaning time—it hadn't been any fault of her own, and Rosalyn was certain that Sophie *knew* it.

Marie looked up from her drawing of a throne, finally, and giggled to herself in wilful ignorance of Rosalyn's silent fury. "She couldn't 'cause Matron caught her messing around in the garden with her hands all filthy, pulling some of the barbed wire off the wall."

Marie smiled smugly in that way she did whenever she got Rosalyn in trouble, which was a frequent occurrence and often just in time to stop Rosalyn from having the chance to do something that she really wanted. The other two girls found it funny and tended to be in exactly the right place to watch without becoming implicated themselves, and they always seemed to know when it was going to happen; it was also one of the reasons why Rosalyn didn't like them.

"I was only out there because *somebody* threw all my clothes in the ditch!" Rosalyn viciously twisted the bit of barbed wire that she was holding carefully, wishing Marie would jump into the ditch in question during a thunderstorm and forget how to swim. "*And* you're the only one who'd gone upstairs before I did after lunch! Just because Matron believed you over me doesn't mean I was 'messing around', so you—"

Sophie, who'd been watching with the owl-like intensity that she often slipped into, lifted the hand that had been resting on the floorboards and pointed at the barbed-wire bundle nestled in Rosalyn's lap and threatening to poke holes in her one clean dress.

"Are you going to finish making that, or will I have to do everything by myself, Ros-*a*-lyn?" She said Rosalyn's name in a slightly sing-song way, her breathy voice making it sound almost insidious.

Glowering at a now smirking Marie, Rosalyn turned her attention back to the bundle of barbed wire in her lap and carried on twisting it carefully into a circle, making sure to keep the barbs poking up and out, battling against the way they tried to turn down and inwards.

Satisfied for now, Sophie drew the final curled line to make the edge of a scroll and stood up, stepping carefully over the scattered drawings until she reached the cabinets by the windows.

Rosalyn looked down at her handiwork as she heard the *click-scrape* of the glass cabinet being opened and smiled to herself at Marie's panicked whisper-yelling about how they weren't supposed to open those cabinets and how Sophie would get them all in so much trouble and to put that candle back before Matron came to check on them and how would they even light it?!

"With a match. I nicked it from Matron's study yesterday when she forgot to lock it." Matter of fact, as though obtaining a match was normal, Sophie walked back to the mess of paper and knelt in the gap she'd left for herself, placing the fat red candle down on the bottom left corner of the paper that held the charter. She took Rosalyn's green crayon from in between drawings of a crown, a tiara, and a four-leafed clover and started to write carefully on the Royal Charter.

With a final bend of metal, Rosalyn locked the strand of wire into place and smiled in triumph, balancing it in front of her on her fingertips to admire it. She opened her mouth to say something about how she was done already but instead just sighed in annoyance as the chore bell invaded the room.

Sophie muttered something very unladylike and rolled the candle until it rested underneath the drapes, hidden, and quickly left the room with Marie, who was very vocal—in whispers, of course—about how they couldn't hide the candle there, and that Rosalyn was sure to rat them out.

For her part, Rosalyn just watched them leave before she placed her newly made crown on her head and stood up to follow the other two and find out what chores she'd been assigned this week. *Just because I probably won't get to wear my crown in the end doesn't make the slightest bit of difference*, she mused. *I made it, after all, so it's mine.*

And for that instant, hidden from the others, she was the Queen.

The chore bell rang again. Rosalyn started, then pulled her crown off and hid it behind the bookshelves; if Matron found it, her hard work would be ruined, and she'd have to start all over again from scratch. With it hidden from sight among the cramped cobwebs, she circled carefully around the drawings and hurried from the room, not about to give the other two time to volunteer her to clean the toilets. With her luck, she'd probably be stuck with doing the laundry for the next hour, which would be a terribly dull way to spend the rest of the afternoon.

※ ※ ※

The butterfly was dead when Rosalyn found it, crumpled in a little heap and flattened like someone had stepped on it. It was a big butterfly, its torn and dusty wings some shade of red that was a little hard to make out.

Beyond repair.

Rosalyn crouched down to pick it up and found she couldn't; if she tried, she would drop the newly washed-and-dried bedsheets piled high in her arms, and then she'd have to wash them all over again and probably miss dinner if Marie had hidden the soaps. The washing basket had vanished whilst Rosalyn had been folding the sheets, with the already-folded ones dumped onto the floor to get dirty. She suspected that had been Marie's doing as well. Knowing Marie's brand of trickery, the basket would be back before Matron could miss it.

Straightening up, Rosalyn carefully stepped over the crushed butterfly and walked down the hall, turning left towards the girl's dormitory when she reached the end— the room for the younger girls was on her right, but she had no reason to go in *there*, nor did she want to. She lifted her elbow to push down the handle and unexpectedly found empty air instead, quickly biting back a curse as her grip on the sheets was momentarily unbalanced. Rosalyn frowned at the door and took a few steps back so that she could actually see the handle over the pile of sheets in her arms, only to find that the door was rather curiously ajar. That was odd indeed. None of the other girls liked having the door open; the last time it had been left wide, five-year-old Olivia had come in and messed up all their things.

Sophie and Marie would have demoted her in the Clover Court if the little kids were allowed to be a part of it, but had instead blamed Rosalyn for allowing it to happen.

Rosalyn had put an upturned bucket over Olivia as payback for that.

She moved closer to shoulder open the door, only to stop short; Sophie was inside, in the process of kneeling down in front of her bed with her back to Rosalyn. The advantage of height allowed her to see that Sophie was holding two things that Rosalyn had never seen in her possession before. In her right hand, she was clutching an empty canning jar filled with small, dull-coloured things in jewel tones, and from her left hung a thin, glass-fronted display case made from dark wood. Her polishing cloths were piled on the floor next to her, lending her an alibi.

Rosalyn had never seen her with anything like that before—Sophie must have hidden them well enough that not even Marie could find them, nosy and meddling as she was. It was strange that Sophie had those, but then again, Sophie was a very strange girl who did things like move all the spiders to be found into one cupboard and then lock people inside for hours at a time. In any case, Rosalyn certainly wasn't about to disturb her, even though her arms were starting to hurt from holding the bedsheets for so long. Instead, she made sure to breathe as quietly as possible as she stared through the cracked door, watching Sophie set the case and the jar onto her bed, then reach into the jar and lift out a large brown butterfly with the sort of care someone would handle fine china teacups.

With her free hand, she lifted the glass lid of the case and placed the butterfly inside, then dipped into the jar again. This time, she pulled out a beetle, shiny and black with an iridescent sheen on its wing-cases, followed by a ladybird. They both went into the case next to the butterfly with the kind of even, measured motions that told Rosalyn they had been placed in a row that was likely perfectly straight and properly spaced out; Sophie was very particular about that sort of thing—it was why she had drawn up the Royal Charter instead of making Rosalyn or Marie do it.

Being careful to avoid the squeaky floorboard that little Olivia always stepped on when she was trying to sneak in, she shifted position to get a better view as Sophie reached off to the side and pulled her arm back with a pincushion in hand. Sophie went still, and just for an instant, it seemed like she was going to turn and catch Rosalyn at the door. She didn't give any sign of noticing her, though, and instead just dropped the pincushion next to the case and withdrew a long pin from the fabric. The pin was promptly pushed into the case through the very dead butterfly underneath it, and the same process was repeated twice more.

Rosalyn wasn't sure how long she stood there, watching Sophie lift bug after dead bug out of the canning jar and into the case to be run through with a pin. It was only once Sophie lifted herself back up to her feet that Rosalyn shifted forwards, pushing open the door with her shoulder and stepping inside; she really had to get a move on, or she'd be in even more trouble than she already was. Having just closed the lid of the case as Rosalyn had come in, Sophie stared at her in an utterly damning silence until Rosalyn dumped the bedsheets onto the bare mattress of her own bed and turned away to start making it before she ran out of time before dinner.

"Don't pretend that you aren't a bug too, Rosalyn."

Rosalyn said nothing, bending down to tuck in the corners of the sheet, smoothing the top flat.

Sophie gave that little huff of maybe irritation, maybe outrage, and Rosalyn heard the sound of a key turning as the case and jar were undoubtedly hidden away again, followed by Sophie's footsteps pacing towards the dormitory door.

"The 'parents' can't see any difference between butterflies and mud-beetles through the glass, you know." And with that, Sophie was gone before Rosalyn could even open her mouth to retort.

The door clicked shut and Rosalyn was left alone in the empty dormitory, feeling the stares of the dead butterflies and beetles and ladybirds from behind their glass-faced home, unwanted and left to collect dust.

※ ※ ※

Supper that night was a careful balancing act of behaving normally whilst pretending that Sophie's barbs from earlier weren't still stinging; her satisfaction was already too unbearable for Rosalyn to stand. Even worse, Marie had figured out that something had happened, and so she was spending every moment watching their faces intently between spoons of soup as she tried to put the pieces together and keep herself in the loop. She looked at Rosalyn more often, so Rosalyn promptly sent a hard kick directly at Marie's leg, vindicated to feel her shoe strike true and catch the flash of pain warp Marie's expression. Served her right for trying to snoop, even if Marie would be looking for revenge as soon as possible. Quickly, Rosalyn tucked her feet in under her chair so Marie wouldn't be able to retaliate without earning Matron's attention. None of them wanted *that*.

Thunder crashed outside as The Clover Court cleared the table ten minutes later; Rosalyn jumped and nearly dropped her pile of crockery, then glanced around to check that no one had noticed, only to see Marie doing the same. Olivia and Susan had seen, but a hard look from Marie was all it took to stop their giggling and send them running from the dining room and up to the nursery, their stamping feet inaudible over the drumming of the torrential rain sluicing down the tall windows. Sophie was in the kitchen; they heard the pantry door creak open before slamming closed a moment after—lately, Hawthorne House had been acting like a building thrice its age.

For Rosalyn, one of the worst parts of the day was cleaning up after supper. They were *supposed* to use a rota, but everyone knew that Sophie wouldn't be caught dead washing up. Matron had given up from the consequences of coercing her to do it, so the dishes had fallen to Marie and Rosalyn regardless of their indignance. The two of them took turns in theory, but Rosalyn was just under a year younger so she had to do most of it—until Matron came by or if Rosalyn was taking too long, at which point Marie would begrudgingly join in with as little compliance as she could get away with. She never gave more than a passing glance at Sophie, who spent her time drying and stacking crockery neatly as if that were the only thing that needed doing, and was therefore the only task worth spending time on.

"I don't see why," Marie said, dunking a dirty plate into the sink at just the right angle to send a wave of freezing water at Rosalyn, who barely dodged, "you're the Queen. I'm older!"

Scummy water dripped from Rosalyn's sleeve, and she waited until Marie was too busy scrubbing to stop her from wringing it out, disgusted, over the sink; the kitchen was just as draughty as the rest of the manor, and Rosalyn wasn't looking to catch cold.

Sophie rolled her eyes and carried a stack of dry plates to the cupboard, letting the door bang open and smirking at Rosalyn as Marie jumped. Marie opened her mouth indignantly, but Sophie spoke up before she could say anything. "In six months, I'll be ten, too." Her tone turned far more taunting than it had been for a while. "If you want to be Queen so badly, why don't you *prove* it?"

Taking her chance, Rosalyn made sure to be careless as she let the soup spoons drop into the wash basin, managing a scoff before Marie cut in over her.

"Prove it how, exactly?" Marie sneered and tossed the washcloth at Rosalyn's face, who ducked as she caught it and began to scrub the cooking pot whilst Sophie smiled serenely.

"That's simple." Her smile wasn't friendly, not at all. "Tell me something I don't already know."

At that, Rosalyn couldn't help but recoil along with Marie; anyone would baulk at an impossible task.

As if she hadn't just proven her own Queenship, Sophie pushed the plates to the back of the cupboard and returned next to Marie, lifting the first of the newly clean bowls and drying it nonchalantly to prompt them to get back to work. None of them wanted to take so long in cleaning that Matron came to check on them; she'd been more uptight than usual these last few days—not even Marie wanted to push her.

"The crown is safe, anyway. I hid it really well." Rosalyn couldn't help but gloat as she finished scrubbing and rinsing the pot.

"You missed a bit! You're gonna get in *trouble*!" Marie never missed an opportunity to dig at her; *of course* she waited until Rosalyn had finished washing the pot before she said anything.

"*You* were meant to do the pot! Maybe I'll just leave it then, see how you like it for once!" Rosalyn nearly threw the pot down, letting it *thud* onto the drying board next to Marie.

"You're already on thin ice, so who do you think she's gonna blame?" Marie's gleeful smugness pervaded the cold kitchen, and Rosalyn blanched, retort forgotten in a flash of disquieting fear. She was already in more than enough trouble with Matron.

"That was your fault, and you know it." Rosalyn hissed after a moment, trying to ignore Sophie's unblinking, analysing gaze as it bore into her. No need to look and give Marie *more* fuel.

The driving rain grew stronger in the gale, battering the manor as even the air in the kitchen hung still in the wake of their words. After what felt like eternity, a throat cleared harshly just as the storm ebbed briefly. The three of them spun as one, and Marie grabbed at the pot in feeble justification, just in case.

"You should be done by now. Get to bed in ten minutes, and I expect this room to be spotless." Matron cut an imposing figure—not even Marie would talk back to her ordinarily.

Rosalyn bit at her chapped lips as Marie's hands tightened on the rim of the pot until her fingers were white, and Sophie shifted subtly in silent mutiny; it was an hour until curfew.

"You have a lot of work to do tomorrow; we're expecting visitors, and you will be on your *best behaviour*. That includes you, Rosalyn."

Rosalyn nodded quickly, even though her getting in trouble had been Marie's fault, and everyone knew it.

With pointed looks at Marie and Sophie, Matron turned on her heel and left, and they listened to her stride through the dining hall and close the double doors firmly.

The moment the coast was clear, the three of them threw themselves into a flurry of work, altercation put to one side in favour of urgent tasks and interesting information. There was no time for sniping at each other. The last time there'd been 'visitors', the now five-year-old Susan had been brought to the doorstep.

❈ ❈ ❈

Rosalyn woke up to someone shaking her shoulder harshly enough to make her cry out. "Wha—?"

"Wake *up*! Hurry up!" Marie, whisper-yelling in her ear. "My clock broke, we're late!"

Oh, crud! How could Rosalyn have miscalculated her revenge so badly? She shoved Marie and the threadbare blanket away and sat up, swinging her legs off her bed. The floorboards were cold, the windows spiderwebbed with frost; it could barely be five in the morning. It wasn't raining yet, but that was a matter of time.

"Where's—?"

"Buying time, hurry up!"

Rosalyn swiped the sleep from her eyes as she stumbled over to the shared wardrobe, yanking the door open and grabbing the only dress of hers that hung there; all the others were hopefully still in the washroom downstairs. It was lilac cotton, not good for cleaning in, but she had no choice. One of Sophie's thick dark blue dresses was missing, and Rosalyn quickly repressed the pearl of jealousy that began to bubble up her throat; green-tinted glasses were no better than rose.

She tugged her dress over her slip and rushed to pull on stockings and shoes, doing up the buckles with one hand and fixing her hair into some semblance of neatness with the other whilst Marie waited at the door, keeping watch. As soon as she was dressed, they ran from the dormitory towards the front of the old manor to relieve Sophie. Hopefully, they wouldn't be in so much trouble that doing the extra chores would be harder than normal.

Half an hour later, Rosalyn shivered as she dragged the broom back and forth, pausing to tug her sleeves over her hands and readjust her grip; the main hall was ice-cold early in the morning, and they weren't allowed to wear coats or gloves indoors. It didn't help that her dress felt so close to damp that Rosalyn couldn't tell if it hadn't dried properly or was just cold—no thanks to Marie for tossing all her clothes out the window. It had taken ages to retrieve them from the garden, and even longer for them to dry enough to keep from dripping on the washroom tiles; her one woollen coat was sodden even after a whole night. She'd checked.

"This is ridiculous, even for *Her* standards!" Marie dunked her mop into the bucket hard enough to make a dull *thud*, glaring at the soap suds as though they personally offended her. "So what if we're having guests? We shouldn't have to wake up early and clean the entire manor if they're only gonna see the front hall and maybe *Her* office." She began to scrub the floor aggressively, and Rosalyn sped up a little; if Marie got close, she'd definitely take the chance to splash her. "And us. I suppose."

"Butterflies or mud-beetles, we're all the same to them." Sophie's murmured comment didn't go unnoticed; Marie snorted derisively, Rosalyn gripped the broom tighter and turned away from them. If the Queen cared enough to speak, Rosalyn couldn't let her see how much her comment stung. She didn't know if Marie saw it, but she was so self-centred that that was unlikely. A shrew of a Princess.

They cleaned in silence for a few minutes, moving down the first floor towards the big staircase. Sophie walked ahead as they drew close, dragging her better-than-Rosalyn's broom behind her. Even the Queen wasn't allowed to be exempt from chores, but that didn't stop her from taking the slightly superior stuff.

"I hope they don't bring another kid. Last thing we need is three Olivias running around, messing up our things." Marie was right, but there was no way that Rosalyn would show that she agreed. Marie let the mop handle drop and Rosalyn swung her broom, knocking it towards the centre of the landing as it fell. "Although"—Marie grabbed the bucket and heaved it closer to the stairs, sloshing water everywhere—"someone older might be worse."

Rosalyn picked the mop up, making a face at the freezing wood, and tossed it into Marie's waiting hand. Her fingers were white. Someone around their age would be best, but that would bring a problem, which Rosalyn thought to point out. "We'd have to make room for another Princess …" A glance at Sophie's turned back. "Maybe reset the Court, start again, re-elect a Queen …" At least then, Rosalyn could have a chance of disrupting their tug-of-war.

Sophie looked back sharply, her brief glare harsher than the wind and rain that was starting to lash down outside and smack against the windows. "No. A new member will join the Court as …" She swept dust between the bannister spokes, turning her broom so it fitted through the gaps without banging. "A Duchess. If she can prove that she deserves the rank of Princess, we'll discuss it, and the Queen will make the final decision."

The two thought it over, Marie still mopping the floor with such surliness that Rosalyn kept an eye on the mophead, cautious for her own stockings. The Queen wasn't at risk, about to get a head start on the godforsaken staircase.

Showers of grit fell down into the main hall from the landing and caught the grey early morning light from the tall windows as Sophie knocked it down.

"Well, alright."

Rosalyn rolled her eyes at Marie's acquiescence, thinking privately that she'd only agreed to get on Sophie's façade of a good side. Rosalyn didn't know why she bothered with this charade—both Queen and Princess saw through it, clear as glass. Pretences of goodwill hardly mattered; the gauntlet was thrown down yesterday, the game had well and truly started. And Rosalyn wasn't reckless like Marie—she was biding her time, waiting until she had an uncontested shot.

"Fine." No need to rock the boat just yet.

Rosalyn reached the stairs and started to sweep the pile of accumulated dust off the ledge with quick, brusque strokes as Sophie walked down, dragging her broom and letting it bump from one step to the next. The wood creaked at Sophie's slight weight and Rosalyn suppressed her wince; with how woodworm-riddled it was, she'd been expecting it to collapse any day now. The staircase and the first floor were utterly infested, but Matron wouldn't hear it—said they were making it up to cause trouble, said they were breeding the repulsive things when Sophie showed her the larvae to prove it wasn't part of their game. The Clover Court didn't understand why she'd think that: what kind of Queen would rule a crumbling castle? What sort of Princesses would put up with such behaviour?

Rosalyn trod as lightly as possible as she stepped down onto the top step, which creaked ominously, just as Marie's mop whipped past where her feet had been. "What d'you think happened? To the new girl?" She turned her head to smile smugly up at her; *nice try, Princess,* but you *missed*.

Marie pointedly ignored her as she carelessly dunked the mop into the bucket again, letting it rest against the rim whilst she rubbed her hands together and blew on them, probably trying to get feeling back.

"I think it was some dreadful accident. So now, there's no one left for her." Rosalyn wanted to know what the other two thought had happened to necessitate visitors—she wasn't going to let it slide without an opinion from them first. Meanwhile, she started sweeping the stairs in earnest, moving as fast as she could but being careful of Marie.

"Or no living relatives wanted her." Sophie had reached the bottom of the stairs, and she dragged her broom to the far end of the entrance hall and began sweeping, her back to the tall, frosted-over windows.

Rosalyn swallowed and took the next step a little more heavily than she intended—Marie hid a giggle against the crook of her elbow as Sophie tilted her head to one side, all faux-concern and empty contrition. "But I thought you *wanted* to discuss this, *Ros*-a-*lyn*. Maybe no one wanted her at all …"

Rosalyn swept the last few steps in stony silence, gritting her teeth and clenching her hands around the broom until her knuckles turned white, determined not to rise to the bait. She wished that she had something to say in return; the alternative was hurling the broom at Sophie's head and risking breaking a window.

"That's dumb. I bet she was in a car crash, and all her family *died*." Rosalyn had never been gladder for Marie's need to one-up Sophie; for once, it worked in her favour.

Sophie rolled her eyes as she pushed the broom underneath the stairs and vanished from sight—Matron would check there for cobwebs, and Sophie liked spiders far too much for anyone's peace of mind. She was making a mound of broken webs just out from underneath the death-trap excuse of a staircase, but as there were no spiders to be seen, Rosalyn started sweeping the pile towards the front door, adding it to the dust from the stairs. As she did, Sophie came and gathered the mess from the landing; the work went faster when she deigned to contribute, and they all wanted to finish quickly.

As glad as she was for Marie's interjection, her idea was still stupid, and so Rosalyn readily took her chance to prove Marie wrong. "An accident like that would kill her, y'know. Or she'd be in hospital for months and months, not dumped here instead."

And with that one suggestion against her, Marie smiled down on Rosalyn and, from her tone, said what she'd probably been desperate to say since Sophie had mentioned it. "But if Sophie's right, you'll have something in common to cry about for sure. Right, Ros-*a*-lyn?"

And Rosalyn thought that she'd break either the broom shaft or her fingers—whichever gave first—and she couldn't bear to look up at Marie and give her the satisfaction.

Marie stifled giggles, and Rosalyn couldn't help but spit out the one theory that she'd thought of but refused to say, blurting it out for the draughty, creaking hall and the Queen to hear, standing witness. "I bet she was in a *fire*! I bet her house burned down with all her family inside and she couldn't save them, and it was all her faul—" Freezing-cold water cut her off, soaking her to the bone as Sophie gave a surprised shout, drenched as well; Marie had upturned the bucket directly above them.

"Tripped."

She hadn't. They all knew it. Rosalyn spluttered and tried to shake the water from her hands and squeeze the worst of it from her dress, already shivering. "Now look at what you've done! If we're not finished soon, we'll all get in trouble, you absolute cow!"

Marie positively skipped down the stairs, letting the bucket clank at her heels. "And who do you think she'll blame? Me, or you two? It was an accident, and you're both still standing around like this place'll sweep itself."

"But—" Rosalyn couldn't believe her audacity.

"I give the orders now!"

Incredulous and wanting confirmation of such a claim—that Sophie had just lost her Queenship to such a one-uppance—Rosalyn spun to stare at the silent, seething Sophie, drenched in water and glaring at Marie with such vitriol that Rosalyn half-expected Marie to combust.

"You would've moved, if you'd known!" Marie's glee was sickeningly self-righteous, and she turned on her heel and strode into the adjoining hallway, dragging the bucket along. They heard the lavatory door creak open, followed by the sound of running water and triumphant humming, barely audible under the sloshing.

Sophie rolled her shoulders and wrung out her two low ponytails in deliberate, slow motions, then went back to sweeping mechanically, ignoring the water and Rosalyn. It was uncanny, methodical, and if she didn't know any better, Rosalyn might mistake her for calm. There wasn't anywhere near enough time for Sophie to run and change into dry clothes without Matron catching her; revenge was surely on the now-Princess's mind, and Rosalyn certainly wasn't going to interrupt and paint a bigger target on her own back.

Queen Marie re-entered the hall, holding the bucket with both hands; it looked heavy. Nothing more was said as they went back to work, the two Princesses gritting their teeth against the cold and trying not to shiver.

❦ ❦ ❦

It was Rosalyn who heard the sharp knock at the front door that evening after a day of mathematics homework and impatient waiting, Rosalyn who ran as silently as she could to fetch Sophie and Marie from the attic, Rosalyn who reached the landing first and watched as Matron pulled the door open to usher inside a tall lady and her charge.

The Clover Court had been using the time before bed to start putting together their attic Throne Room, and so it was lucky that they had caught the knock at all; Rosalyn had only heard it because she'd been sent to retrieve the crown from its hiding place in the living room. She'd slipped past Matron's office and had been halfway up the highest staircase when she'd heard the knock—after a few years, she'd learned how to run quietly on the floorboards. She'd burst into the Throne Room, dropped the crown for Marie to wear later onto the chair they'd chosen as the Throne, and had made it down to the first landing just in time.

The formally dressed woman spoke to Matron in an undertone—umbrella in hand—whilst not one, but *two* girls huddled behind her, holding a battered suitcase each and staring around at the gloomy, drab interior of Hawthorne House. They looked about the same age as Rosalyn; wet hair and pinched faces, raindrops pearled on their coats. She heard the soft creak of Marie's feet a few paces behind her at the same time that Sophie placed her hand lightly on the bannister with a suddenness that made Rosalyn's breath catch.

Matron's voice drifted up from below, and the smaller of the new girls looked back at her, turning away from staring up at the first-floor landing. Her eyes were empty hollowed-out husks. "Heather and Willow Phillips, you will be living here from now on. You will behave and do as you're told; ask the other girls for the rules. Your dormitory is on the second floor, third door on the left."

"New Duchesses?" Rosalyn breathed the question, heard the Queen's answer.

"Course."

Chapter Two – Charter

No one was supposed to be around, as far as Rosalyn knew, and so she was taken by surprise when the door to the first-floor lavatory creaked open and Willow slipped inside, dark green dress dusty and one long plait missing the ribbon. She didn't even seem to notice that the door to the far-left cubicle was closed, didn't seem to notice that she wasn't alone, that Rosalyn was watching her over the edge.

Standing up on the toilet cistern, Rosalyn held her breath, hoping that the other girl wouldn't pay attention to the cubicles or look in one of the mirrors at the right angle to spot her. After all, Willow would tell Heather, who would almost certainly tell Matron that Rosalyn had been seen standing on the toilet cistern with her hands up in the ceiling tiles and was so very obviously Up To No Good, Honestly! Never mind that they'd all get a severe scolding for messing with the ceiling tiles, at the very least; Matron had decided a few months ago that if one of them knew something, there was a good chance it would be common knowledge by bedtime. If the other two found out that Rosalyn had been hiding her things above the left-cubicle toilet ... Well, there would be absolute hell to pay, for one.

She didn't want to think about what could happen if they got wind of it, and so she very carefully didn't, instead watching as Willow stamped her feet and shook out her dress with horrified disgust plastered all over her face. A spider about the size of a thimble fell from the lace-trimmed hem and scuttled off across the floor, vanishing into the shadow cast by the door. Privately, Rosalyn thought that this display was a significant improvement of sorts over the blankness she usually wore like a shroud; *any* personality was better than the ashy hollowness they'd all come to expect from Willow.

"Ugh! What is *wrong* with her?"

Oh! That explained where Willow had been since just after breakfast; Sophie must have finally managed to lock her in her favourite cupboard, the one with all the spiders. It had only taken two weeks to happen; Rosalyn had almost thought that Sophie had finally been outwitted. Now it seemed she'd seized her chance earlier after Matron had physically hauled Willow away from her books. Even now, there was a battered storybook tucked under her arm, a spider crawling from inside the spine only to be shaken off and stamped on moments later.

Maybe they should just start checking that damned cupboard whenever anyone goes missing, barring Sophie.

"Stupid spiders!" A page fell loose from the book; Willow bent down to retrieve it and stilled in shock, staring at something in the centre cubicle as her fingers froze in mid-air, barely brushing the page. Puzzled, Rosalyn followed her gaze and leaned forwards slightly, shifting her weight carefully on the ceramic cistern as she looked over the wall into the middle cubicle. A fine-linked necklace chain was trailing from the toilet bowl, most of it barely visible from the disgusting mass that it was wedged in and under; Rosalyn only noticed the part that had been spared when the light glinted off the silver and reflected on the tiled, wet floor around the toilet.

The page crunched as Willow picked it up and clenched her hand into a fist before walking the few feet to the middle-cubicle toilet in slow, disbelieving steps, her patent shoes dragging on the tiles, the spiders forgotten. Rosalyn could only watch from above, not daring to make a sound as Willow pinched the chain between finger and thumb and pulled, pulled until it came free.

With a sickening squelch, the pendant on the other end jerked out from the mess in the toilet bowl and swung in the air, dripping scummy water everywhere and marking Willow's dress and shoes with dark spots. Rosalyn had never seen the pendant in much detail before, as Willow insisted on wearing it constantly, tucked under her blouse or dress so that only a slight lump could be noticed. She could see now that it was a locket, the kind with an engraving on the front and a hinge on the side, but the front was badly dented, and the hinge was bent. Rosalyn wasn't certain that the locket would be able to open properly now, but that wasn't *her* problem. Knowing the others, the new girl's locket hadn't been like that before.

And then she went very still and looked up at Rosalyn, her scowling face darkened like Rosalyn had never seen before. "How long have—"

"It wasn't me, I swear!" Rosalyn hastily pulled her hands down from the gap in the ceiling tiles, stumbling over her words in her haste to get them out. "I didn't know that locket was there! I didn't take it or put it there or have the idea to! And—and I would never do that anyway, so—"

"And it wasn't you who filled Marie's pillowcase with thumbtacks either, I expect? Oh, of course, my mistake, you would never ever *ever* do something mean like that..." Her glare was scathing; Rosalyn was nearly intimidated by the stick-thin girl with a ruined locket and cobwebs in her hair.

"That was *necessary*! You're just a Duchess, you wouldn't understand!"

"I bet you didn't know that I saw you messing with the pillowcases, just like you didn't know that I could see you just now!" Willow was too hurt to be triumphant.

Rosalyn watched the locket's chain tremble with her efforts to keep her voice at least a little hushed, even though their voices echoed in the cramped lavatory.

"You're always sneaking and spying, thinking you're so much better than me and Heather and acting like the Queen you're not ..." Willow sent the toilet a disgusted look, then turned it on Rosalyn. "You wouldn't be hiding your things if you hadn't done this, so get off your throne, oh-high-and-mighty-*Princess*, before I *make* you!"

It was like the other girl didn't even realise that Rosalyn had the higher ground, so she made sure to look down at her, leaning over and resting her hands on the cubicle partition.

"I didn't take your stupid locket, so maybe you should go and disrespect whoever actually did it, instead of just blaming the closest person! Or maybe, just maybe, you should earn your place to be a Princess—it's gotta be a better life than you deserve right now ..." Rosalyn realised with a start that she was beginning to sound like Marie, but in that moment, she didn't care how nastily the words were twisting in her mouth. She wanted Willow to hurt. She wanted Willow to listen to her, as was her right as a Princess. She wanted to storm out in a flurry of self-righteousness, but she couldn't risk Willow ruining her stuff before she could find a new hiding place for them. Now that Willow knew her secret, she had to relocate her few precious things before the others found them or Matron confiscated them.

Willow stamped her foot, punctuating her fury-hurt words with the way the noise reverberated against the tiles, bouncing off the walls and floor. "Fine! *Fine*! Maybe I will, then, and you'll all be sorry! I thought you were nicer than them ... Looks like I was wrong to hope for the best, what with all the spying and stealing my things." The paper in her fist tore as her fingers broke through it; the book tucked under her arm slipped a little bit.

"Why would I help the Queen? I'm trying to earn her crown, not make sure she keeps it! And I don't want Sophie taking it up again!" Something crashed outside as the wind picked up, howling around the corners of the House. It sounded a bit like the door to the old shed in the garden had swung out and slammed against the wall. The lavatories were on the first floor at the back of the manor, so it was either the shed or the branches of the tree that grew behind the building. Rosalyn didn't know for sure, but it wouldn't surprise her if that was the Hawthorn in question that gave the orphanage its name.

"It probably wasn't Sophie who did this, and if it was Marie, then you helped her. Me and Heather've done nothing to you, so let's see how you and Sophie and Marie like it to taste your own medicine!" With that, Willow gave the locket a good shake over the toilet to get the worst of the muck off, then turned on her heel and left the cubicle, not even looking at Rosalyn.

"It really wasn't me, honest!"

"You're a liar, Ros-*a*-lyn."

With that mimicry of how the others taunted her, Willow stormed out, pulling the door shut behind her; it banged back open a little, and Rosalyn heard a few stifled, furious sobs before Willow ran from the first-floor loos, her footsteps creaking towards the dormitories.

Well, Rosalyn thought to herself as she lifted the tile up again, *it seemed like the Clover Court had a new potential Princess.* It would fall to her to inform the Court of the changing stakes, and bear Marie's insufferable smugness that her foul trick had been the catalyst to push Willow into joining the Clover Court properly.

Once her handful of precious things were safe in her arms, she moved the ceiling tile back into place and clambered down from the cistern, leaving the lavatory in search of a better hiding spot. Perhaps the attic? But their Throne Room was there, so she would have to hide her things well and quickly. And she pretended as hard as she could not to notice the strange feeling that twisted her insides into knots when she stepped over the dots of water droplets that were left dark on the floorboards.

Sometime later, the dead spider on the bathroom floor would find itself in Sophie's possession, and then in a jar kept carefully secret from the Clover Court.

❧ ❧ ❧

For the rest of the day, Rosalyn tried to keep an eye on Willow without the girl noticing, which was harder than it seemed; Heather stuck to her side like glue, and the two of them refused to even talk to Rosalyn. They turned away whenever she approached, Willow glaring daggers at her over the pages of her book whilst Heather tried to fix the locket, giving her glowering, hostile stares until Rosalyn had no choice but to walk away.

The Phillips sisters had hidden themselves away during the entire afternoon. Rosalyn had searched all over for them—with the exception of Matron's study—and had had to endure Marie's smirks and giggling whenever they crossed paths on the stairs or in one of the halls or in the dormitory; she had even checked underneath all the beds, just in case. All the same, she was careful in how she looked about for them, making sure to tread lightly like Sophie did whenever she sneaked up on someone. She just wanted to see what Willow was doing and find out ahead of time if she was planning anything. The Duchess had sworn revenge for the perceived slight, and so Rosalyn would be a true fool to not take her seriously.

If she was noticed, there was no way that Heather wouldn't immediately tattle on her to Willow, and then Rosalyn would have to convince them both of a current lack of plans against them and of her innocence in the lavatory incident. Rosalyn also wanted to find some concrete evidence that the trick had been Marie's doing, if only to get her to admit it in front of Willow. Marie would have been the prime suspect even if Rosalyn hadn't been certain it was her; directly damaging a family heirloom wasn't Sophie's style, and besides, succeeding in locking Willow inside that spider cupboard had probably satisfied her. For today, at least.

It didn't matter that Rosalyn hadn't been the one to steal Willow's locket and ruin it—Willow thought she had.

It wasn't until just before supper when Rosalyn finally found them in the laundry room, heads bent together as they discussed something in hushed tones in the corner. Willow's book was propped up on her knees—Rosalyn could see that she was reading a guide to common household insects of Britain—and Heather was sitting next to her, leaning over to fiddle with something in her sister's lap. They hadn't noticed her yet, so Rosalyn took those precious few moments to tilt up onto her tiptoes to try to discern what Willow was hiding. She couldn't get a good look at it. They seemed just as angry as before, but there was something satisfied in the set of Willow's shoulders that made her stomach twist uncomfortably, so Rosalyn backed away and walked quickly down the hallway to her left towards the main staircase, just as their heads began to rise.

There was clearly no getting through to Willow, and Rosalyn suspected that they knew of her attempts to figure out what they were doing; finding them in the laundry room had been a double-edged sword. Trying to find out more information would be inviting trouble, and so she deliberately didn't seek them out after cleaning up the dishes from supper, tracking down Olivia and Susan instead; Rosalyn's new plan needed them.

When she found the two younger girls, they were playing with the old rocking horse in the nursery; from the looks of it, trying to ride sidesaddle without slipping off. Rosalyn leaned against the doorframe and knocked on the wood to draw their attention, blinking at their scowls. It wasn't like she'd filled *their* pillows with thumbtacks or anything.

"D'you want to learn hopscotch? I saw you trying to play it at the schoolhouse."

Susan wound her fingers in the horse's bedraggled mane and jumped to push herself back up onto the horse's seat, Olivia grabbing onto the head to stop it rocking too much before she frowned at Rosalyn.

"But you said you didn't wanna play with us, and you and the others keep being really mean to me."

"And me! And you … and …" Susan's shoes tapped against the floor as she slid off the rocking horse, and she stopped talking, trying to untangle her fingers from the mane.

When she didn't start talking again, Olivia piped up. "If you teach us, you gotta be nice. No buckets."

With a shrug, Rosalyn agreed easily enough—she needed Olivia and Susan on her side, at least for now—they weren't part of the Court, but they lived in the castle, so if they 'accidentally' affected the game, Rosalyn couldn't be held at fault.

They couldn't go outside to play on the front drive because the ground was too wet to make a hopscotch grid; instead, Rosalyn took the white chalk from the stash in the Throne Room and drew out a grid on the floorboards of the hallway by the dormitories. Of course, they wouldn't be able to play hopscotch outside under ordinary circumstances—Matron didn't allow them to take chalk or crayons out of the manor—but she neglected to tell the two little ones that there was another reason for choosing this corridor to play in. There was only one way into the dormitories, and so Willow would *have* to walk past if she wanted to try something with Rosalyn's bed or personal things. As long as Rosalyn was careful and paid attention, she would be able to hear Matron scolding the others downstairs before bedtime, and would hopefully be able to wipe away the chalk before she came upstairs and caught them marking up the floor.

Halfway through Olivia's turn on the hopscotch, Sophie wandered around the corner and gave them all a steady, measured stare, particularly Rosalyn.

"The chalk's for the Court, and they were about to get us all in trouble," Rosalyn justified herself hastily.

Sophie only glanced down at the hopscotch grid. "The boxes are uneven. I shan't play until you fix them."

Too busy trying to play hopscotch than listen to their conversation, Olivia hopped to square number six, wobbled, and stamped her other foot down so she didn't fall. Rosalyn opened her mouth, only for Sophie to cut in over her. "You missed number seven. You're out."

Olivia was about to protest, but Willow rounded the corner and stopped short upon seeing the four of them—two Princesses, two common children. She had her book under one arm and a small tin in her hand; it was unlabelled, unfortunately, but it looked rusty and dented. Was this what Heather had been tinkering with earlier? Rosalyn wanted to claim her innocence with regard to the damaged locket, but she couldn't possibly do that now—Sophie was there, watching Willow unblinkingly, and so were Susan and Olivia, peering at her curiously. The two five-year-olds had been interested in the new girls, but Heather and Willow had brushed them off until they gave up, like they had with the full Clover Court. It only took a few moments for Willow to cave and run away, leaving Rosalyn on the other end of Sophie's unrelenting gaze.

Repressing a shudder, she turned her attention to Olivia, still standing on the hopscotch grid. "You need to start again. Here, pass me the puck." Olivia blinked in confusion, and Rosalyn clarified. "The checkers piece, give it here."

"Oh!" Olivia kicked at the game piece, missed, and tried again amid Susan's giggles, having to kick it four or five times until it bumped against Rosalyn's shoe. Rosalyn grabbed the piece and threw it into Susan's lap, who clumsily scooped it up, then got to her feet and began to approach the hopscotch board. Rosalyn hid a smile at Sophie's huff of annoyance, and the other Princess turned abruptly to follow after Willow, clearly losing interest in needling Rosalyn.

Good.

Rosalyn walked on eggshells for the rest of the evening, managing to wipe up and hide all trace of the hopscotch game and convince the younger girls not to tell. It hadn't been difficult—all she'd needed to do was remind them that they weren't supposed to mark up the floors and ask them if Matron would *really* care who had done the drawing when the two of them had been the ones playing on it. And it was a good thing, too, that she'd ended the game early, for Matron had come to check on them prematurely. Willow had tattled on her and Sophie, who had surely denied involvement for Matron to be in such a foul mood by the time she'd reached the dormitories.

Rosalyn had looked down at her shoes, denied anything to do with hopscotch or chalk on the floor, and had taken the slap that she knew was coming—no doubt Willow would have had it worse for lying …

Nonetheless, Sophie would now be looking for revenge on the Duchess.

Chapter Three – Sceptre

The next morning, Rosalyn found out what Willow and Heather had been planning, when she went to put her indoor shoes on and something squished under her fingertips. She looked to see something shifting inside them.

She quickly checked to see if anyone had noticed her predicament. Sophie was brushing her hair on the bed next to her own. Marie, already dressed, was sitting on her bed and giving deliberately unhelpful suggestions to a panicking Heather—her blouses had gone missing, apparently. Willow's bed was to Rosalyn's back; she glanced back to see Willow sitting still, doing up the catch to her locket's chain as she watched Rosalyn with a tight smile.

No one except Willow had noticed yet, and so Rosalyn looked back down and casually upturned her shoes, trying her best to swallow down the bile that rose up as what must surely be dozens of maggots fell in a fleshy rain, pattering onto the floorboards. The pile quickly slumped apart, revealing what she now realised was a mixture of woodworm and larvae wriggling in all directions.

"Ugh!" She couldn't stop the exclamation of disgust, and all conversation stopped in lieu of staring at the things inching under her bed and dropping down the cracks between the floorboards. Her stomach rolled, and she had to fight back a wave of nausea from the sight and smell. Belatedly, she knocked her shoes together, and a few more fell out and instantly became part of the dispersing mass.

Sophie stood and put her hairbrush away. "You're lucky I didn't tell on you to Matron," she stated, looking through Rosalyn to Willow, sitting smugly behind her, "for sneaking out in the middle of the night. As if I wouldn't notice." *You owe me* went unsaid, as did the obvious threat she now held over Willow. Not giving Willow a chance to reply, Sophie walked to the door, easily avoiding the woodworm.

"I never did that, Sophie!" Willow called after her, but the target of her words was already gone, so she stood and walked quickly to the door, jumping over the carpet of maggots and woodworm to avoid the worst of them. "Come on, Heather! It's nearly time for breakfast, and karma makes me hungry." She tossed her hair and left, leaving Rosalyn to stare at the larvae that had just been in her shoes.

She had nearly put them on without checking. She had nearly forgotten about Willow's inevitable plan for revenge. As if reading her mind, Marie laughed, covering her mouth with one hand as she backed away towards the dormitory door, crushing a maggot that got underfoot. "Better clean those up, Ros-*a*-lyn, 'fore you get in trouble for it. It would be easier if—" She stopped to giggle. "If only you'd worn them first ..."

Rosalyn was left to stare in growing despair at the carpet of larvae. There were so many ... how on earth was she supposed to get rid of them? At least half had vanished into the floorboards like water draining through a tiny gap. She quickly wrote off any chance of finding those. The smell truly was awful; every time she caught a whiff, she nearly gagged. She distantly heard Marie knocking on the other dormitory door to make sure the younger girls were awake. When had Marie left the room?

There wasn't anywhere for her to put her shoes to wipe down the insides—the floor wasn't safe, and Matron might find out if they touched her sheets—so Rosalyn double-checked for any more woodworm before she slid them on and did up the buckles. She would just have to give her stockings two washes, rather than one. No longer at risk of the maggots touching her feet, Rosalyn stared down at the mess, trying to figure out what to do about it.

A hand thrust into the air in front of her, fingers wrapped around a rusty tin can. "Here. Willow got them up here in this." Heather was standing at the foot of the bed—Rosalyn hadn't noticed her move. "So you should be able to fit them all back in. Toss 'em out the window or something."

"It wasn't me!" The words blurted out of her mouth, and she tasted bile against her tongue. "I dunno what Willow told you, but it wasn't—" Her protest stuttered and died as she saw Heather's eyes harden into a flat, unimpressed look.

"I won't cover for you if you're late."

The tin fell into her lap, and she glanced down at the sudden contact, hearing Heather stride from the dormitory as she did so.

Rosalyn looked around in the sudden silence.

A few thumps came from across the hall, from the younger girls' dormitory. After a moment, she looked back down and stood up, holding the tin, placing her feet carefully to avoid the maggots. It took some jumping and delicate positioning, but she made her way over to the door and closed it; she didn't want Olivia or Susan seeing what had happened and tattling on her to Matron.

The maggots hadn't spread across the whole room, thankfully, but they filled the space between Sophie's bed and her own, as well as underneath it, and she could see some crawling towards Willow's. There was no time to waste, and so she pulled the neckline of her dress up over her nose and mouth before crouching down to start scooping up the woodworm closest to her, using the lid as a shovel. Those that had escaped through the floorboards weren't her problem, and she didn't bother with the handful that she spotted crawling under Willow's bed.

The other girl had made an amateur mistake to let Rosalyn clean them up unsupervised.

After she'd gathered the majority, she balanced the lid on the can whilst she looked for the rest, double-checking under the beds of the Clover Court proper—this particular spat was with Willow, and she didn't want to give the others an excuse to join in. There were a couple crawling near one of Marie's bedposts, so they joined the rest in the can with some reluctance on her part. She decided to check under Heather's bed as well, just in case, since Willow's sister had been nice enough to give her a way to clean up, even if she hadn't believed in Rosalyn's innocence. She saw neither woodworm nor maggots, and she was about to get back up when something curved caught her eye, enticing her to lean in for a better look.

There was an enamelled brooch underneath Heather's bed, securely pinned to the mattress in the shadow of a bed slat and relatively well-hidden from sight—Rosalyn had only found it because she'd happened to look at exactly the right angle as she'd ducked her head to see under the bedframe. The brooch was a lovely little thing, oval-shaped and elegant, and Rosalyn made sure to remember where it was, in case it went missing later. After all, family heirlooms had been the untouchable property of each Court member until yesterday morning, and Heather wasn't yet a proper Princess—technically. Willow's reaction had given Rosalyn the credit of Willow's official enrolment in the Court, and so there was no reason for her to also give Heather a push.

Well, there was no real need to dwell on Heather's secrets for the time being. Worried about being late for breakfast, Rosalyn grabbed the tin and swiftly dumped the contents into Willow's bed, then smoothed the sheets back down and left the room. She'd hide the tin can in the spider cupboard at the top of the stairs on her way to the dining room, and hopefully she wouldn't be in *too* much trouble for tardiness.

※ ※ ※

"How many arches should we have?"

"Five, obviously. One for each of us, stupid."

"I was just making sure, Your *Highness*." Rosalyn rolled her eyes at Marie's back and began to draw the first of five arches on the floor in white chalk, using the toe of her shoe to scrub away the red chalk where it intersected. The red royal carpet had been one of the first things that they'd drawn and coloured in on the dusty floorboards so that the Queen didn't have to walk on the 'dirt' like everyone else; Marie had stood imperiously in the doorway until it was done, and Sophie had made Willow and Rosalyn fill in most of it with all the red chalk that they had.

She had been in the attic for around an hour. Matron had gone to the village for something important that they weren't allowed to know the details of, and so the Clover Court had rushed through their chores and run up to the attic as soon as possible. The attic had been chosen as their Throne Room just before the two Duchesses—one of them now a Princess—had arrived. Matron didn't care to give them more than a scolding if they went up there, as long as they didn't get dirty. They'd pinned the Royal

Charter to the inside of the door, and the Roster was going to be added to it, just as soon as they'd worked out a way to keep it fancy and official and still be able to move names around as the rankings changed. Sophie had suggested writing Rosalyn's name at the very bottom, since she'd 'never become Queen', but Willow had smashed a plate and made it look like Sophie's fault before Queen Marie could agree, and so Rosalyn's name had stayed on a separate slip of paper like all the others.

The entire Court was in the attic during their unexpected free time, even Heather, who was standing by the door and watching them all in muted disapproval, arms folded and shoulders hunched. She kept glancing to the big wooden chair that they had decided was their throne and biting her lip anxiously—Rosalyn didn't understand why until she followed her gaze.

It took her a moment to work it out; Heather was actually looking underneath the throne, where Marie had placed a wooden hammer that she'd run through with nails stolen from the door to the shed outside. The shed door had been torn from its hinges during yesterday's gale; they'd all run out to have a look the moment the rain had stopped before Matron could tell them not to. Going out to see the broken door hadn't been worth the mud they'd scrubbed off their shoes, nor the trouble they got in.

Rosalyn didn't know where Marie had found the hammer, or how she'd sneaked it into the manor without the rest of the Court noticing, but would never admit that to Marie by asking her. And Rosalyn certainly wasn't about to cave and try to convince Sophie to tell her how Marie had done it. Better just to pretend she knew and not question how or why the Queen had taken a hammer for herself. That kind of thing was better not speculated on too much.

Willow had no such reservations and frowned when she saw it—or rather, when her knee knocked against the handle and she bent down to see what it was. It was Willow's job to decorate the throne and fill in the outlines that Marie had already drawn, and so she'd ended up sitting on the floor with the skirt of her dress full of all the yellow and orange crayons that could be found, colouring the arms, sides and back of the chair with ornate swirls that she was trying to make as close to gold as possible.

She frowned as she saw the hammer, and Rosalyn watched her look around quickly, her head jerking from Marie, to Sophie, to Rosalyn herself, her eyes wide with fear and disbelief. Rosalyn turned just enough to scrutinise their reactions; Sophie was still calmly drawing the design of their Royal Crest, not pausing at all, and Marie was smirking from where she leaned against a beam.

"The Queen's Sceptre isn't for little Princesses to be concerned about. *Right*, Princess Willow?" Marie pushed off from the beam and strode down the path of red chalk—Rosalyn moved off the royal carpet just as Marie swung a foot her way—approaching Willow.

Willow swallowed, twisting her hands in her skirt as she began to lean back, kicking the sceptre away like it had burnt her. "Right! But why ... why does it need to have nails in it?"

Marie rolled her eyes as she reached the throne and turned to sit in it, crossing her legs and glaring down at Willow imperiously. "For ornamentation, obviously. Anything else would've fallen out."

Over by the door, she heard Heather scoff.

"Pushpins or thumbtacks wouldn't fall out, not unless you knocked them really hard." Rosalyn hadn't realised that she'd voiced the thought aloud until the two by the throne turned to look at her, one thankful, one incredulous-covering-annoyance.

"But I didn't have any of those, did I now, Ros-*a*-lyn?" Marie was smiling sickly-sweet at her, all honey-coated venom. "Matron confiscated them all after they were found in my pillowcase, but of course you wouldn't know *anything* about that, now would you?"

Rosalyn rolled her eyes, not bothering to pretend that little trick hadn't been her handiwork. "That's not the point! You still coulda got them if you really wanted to ..."

A slight movement caught their attention. Sophie was reaching out slowly, staring at a dark brown Something crawling on the floorboards not two feet from her, her drawings of the Crest forgotten in a stack next to her. Heather made a disgusted noise that Rosalyn wholeheartedly agreed with, Marie rolling her eyes with a muttered diatribe. Sophie definitely overheard, but she ignored their revulsion and cupped the crawling thing in her hands. Closing her fingers around it carefully, she lifted it up slowly and watched her prisoner in fascination. To avoid looking at Marie, Rosalyn watched too, and so she saw Princess Sophie spread her fingers enough to let slivers of light into her cupped hands, just enough to let the dark bug's spindly legs scrabble through the cracks between her thin fingers.

She needed to change the subject, and quickly, before Marie focused on her transgression. Again. "When are we gonna get the clovers? We can't be the Royal Clover Court without any clovers."

"Soon as it stops raining, Ros-*a*-lyn." The five of them turned their heads as one to glance out of the attic window; the rain was still sheeting down, and there was a distant rumble of thunder. Wind whistled around the manor house; Rosalyn wasn't sure if she was imagining the draught.

"It'll be all muddy ... the proper clovers can wait for now. Willow, draw us a row of clovers." Willow glared at Rosalyn, but Rosalyn didn't care—she *barely ever* got to order people around, so Willow would just have to deal with it this time. It was only fair.

"Why don't *you* draw them, Ros—"

"I outrank you!" Rosalyn got up and went over to the table behind Sophie, where they were keeping all of the supplies for creating the Throne Room properly. Before Willow could protest again, she grabbed the green crayon off the dusty surface and threw it in Willow's general direction, watching as Marie had to quickly duck out of the way of its trajectory. The crayon clattered onto the floor behind the throne, and Willow leaned over to grab it mulishly before it rolled away.

"Watch it, Princess! I'll push you down the stairs if you get wax on my dress."

From the corner of her eye, Rosalyn noticed Heather's frown deepen.

Although Marie was the Queen, some retorts simply had to be given, lest she think *too* highly of herself. "Wax on your dress would improve it." Rosalyn had been about to sit down on the table, but Sophie turned her head and looked from Rosalyn to the half-finished arches pointedly, and so she huffed and pushed away from the table to get back to work.

"Just for that, you'll be getting the shoddiest clover we can find." Marie glared at her and reached down to pluck a white crayon from the pile in Willow's skirt, twirling it in her fingers.

"But shoddiness suits you so well, Marie ..." Sophie's whispery voice was calm and monotone, as if stating a fact.

"Silence, Princess! You're not the Queen anymore!"

Sophie didn't even deign to look at the Queen on her throne, instead watching the bug in her hands scrabble for purchase. Contemplatively, she tilted her head as her fingers clenched steadily until the little wriggling legs went limp. "For now. I will have the Crown by the time we gather the clovers."

"Matron's never gonna let us in the garden at this rate, not after that stupid stunt you pulled with the shed." Heather finally spoke for the first time in an hour, staring daggers at Marie, having correctly chosen the Queen as the one at fault. "And to do what, exactly? Pluck bits of weeds from the garden? Maybe fetch more nails? Would you like some bits of grenade shrapnel from the Great War, since you wanna act like you're some kind of Queen?"

Willow opened her mouth urgently, already beginning to raise her hands, but Heather ignored her more sensible sister and spoke louder.

"This is completely ridiculous! There's nothing wrong with games and make-believe, but can't you see how wretched you all are? Throwing family mementos in the loo, playing cruel tricks, making sure each other get beatings for being in the wrong place? All because you're *bored*? You are *children* playing to amuse yourselves, not some mediaeval court from the Dark Ages!" She stormed forwards into the shocked silence, polished patent shoes striking the floor and smudging the white chalk into the red as she crossed over it, ruining Rosalyn's hard work. At this rate, she would run out of red chalk from fixing mistakes. "None of you even realise just how awful it's become, do you? And now you've forced Willow into playing your sick, twisted game …"

Over by the throne, Willow was frozen where she sat as her sister approached like a furious teacher apprehending unruly schoolchildren. Rosalyn turned her head to watch Heather advance, too stunned to do anything else. Heather stood with her back straight and her hands clenched into tight fists that trembled with anger, towering over the Queen as though she wasn't just a lowly Duchess, speaking out of line.

"I'm older than all of you, and I'm telling you that you've gone too far! Enough is enough—your 'Clover Court' is barbaric, and so are all of you! I'll have no part in it, and neither will Willow!"

For a long, awful moment, everything stood still. The rain, falling heavy now, picked up; thunder crashed in the distance.

Rosalyn couldn't breathe.

The white crayon snapped in Marie's fingers, the two halves falling to the ground as she stood from her throne and grabbed a handful of Heather's meticulously brushed hair with one hand and the sleeve of her dress with the other.

Rosalyn saw Willow's head jerk up in alarm. She saw Marie shove Heather to one side as hard as she could. She saw Heather throw out her hands to break her fall. She landed hard and grazed her palms. She saw Marie grab the hammer from under the throne and raise it high over the fallen Duchess. Saw Marie hold it up for one long, terrible moment. Saw her smile sweetly and let it swing gently down again. Saw it drop onto the floorboards with a thud-*thud* of wood as she let go of the handle. Saw her reach up to take hold of her crown.

"You want to tell us what to do? Want to act like you can rule us?" The Queen's voice was chillingly sweet, forcing Rosalyn to suppress a shiver. "Then *be the Queen*."

Sophie rose to her feet silently. Marie took her crown off. Sophie unclasped her hands and beckoned to Rosalyn. The bug dangled from the fingers of her other hand. Marie lowered the crown down to Heather's head, floating it in front of her eyes. Sophie began to walk forwards as Rosalyn scrambled to comply and stand and follow. Marie flipped the crown so that the barbed wire pointed down.

"Go on, Duchess. Be the Queen."

Heather looked up, disbelieving. Sophie gestured for Rosalyn to go to the throne. Rosalyn bit her lip and obeyed; Sophie's eyes were colder than ever before.

"I don't—"

Marie placed the crown on Heather's head. She reached out again, over Heather. She grabbed Rosalyn's arm and yanked her forwards. Heather turned her head, looked up at Rosalyn.

Rosalyn saw her eyes widen. Rosalyn saw Marie place Rosalyn's own hands on the crown. The crown she'd made. Rosalyn saw Marie smile sweet as honey. Rosalyn felt Sophie come up behind her. Rosalyn saw Sophie's corpse-cold hands reach around to press ever-so-gently on her wrists. Rosalyn felt the broken legs of the dead moth caress the back of her hand. Rosalyn saw Heather's face pale in anticipation. There was red chalk dust in her hair now, from Rosalyn's fingers.

And Rosalyn pushed the crown down onto, into Heather's head.

Marie crowed in open delight as Heather let out a short, almost muted scream of pain, the barbs digging into her skin and scalp, drawing bright red blood. Rosalyn wanted to let go, but Sophie's hands were still there, resting on hers. She couldn't lift it up. So she pushed it down harder and watched the blood bead up and steadily drip in a ring around Heather's head. Another crown to compliment the Queen's.

"Stop ... stop it!" Heather's voice was thick with suppressed tears, but Marie just spoke over her.

"No. Princess Willow, come here."

Willow stood woodenly, Rosalyn's crayons falling out of her skirt and rolling every which way across the floorboards. The Queen beckoned, and she trudged the few steps over to where they stood guard around the fallen Duchess.

Princess Sophie spoke before the Queen could, her tone firm and insistent, her question rhetorical. "Well, what are you waiting for? Punish the Duchess."

Willow lifted her hands slowly and brought them up to rest in front of Rosalyn's; their fingertips touched. Her hands were clammy and trembling on the crown, her head was shaking slowly from side to side, her two plaits swaying. And Rosalyn felt the crown sink a little deeper in.

Rosalyn was sorry, she was sorry, she was so sorry, but she couldn't say it.

Sophie lifted her hands up and stepped back, apparently satisfied. Rosalyn could still feel the press of her touch, ghost-cold and lingering. A moment later, Willow had snatched her hands back and was bolting towards the attic door, breaking into a sprint as soon as she got past Sophie.

The crown slid away from under Rosalyn's hands as Heather's eyes closed and she slumped to the floor in a faint, motionless between Rosalyn and the Queen. The three Royals stared for a moment, before the Queen reached down to yank her crown off, pulling out a few strands of blonde hair along with it.

"That should be mine. You don't deserve it." Sophie's decree was soft, monotone.

Marie stepped over Heather's unconscious form and shoved Rosalyn to the side, ignoring her grunt of surprise and pain as she fell back, her hands slamming into the floorboards and pain twinging up to her elbows. Not even a second later, Marie had snatched the dead moth from Sophie's dangling fingers and thrown it to the floor, stamping on it hard before Sophie could stoop to pick it up.

"Oh, but I deserve it even more now! You might have pushed their hands down, but I'm in charge here, and we both know it. All *you're* good for is collecting spiders and being weird and creepy, it's prob'ly why you stared at your Grandpa's dead body for a week before people found out about him! You're sick, messed up in the head. I'd be surprised if you didn't dissect him too, or stick pins through him!"

Sophie was silent, statue-still; Rosalyn wasn't even sure she was breathing. And then her eyes snapped up from the crushed moth to glare at Marie, and the Queen recoiled out of some buried instinct; they had never seen Sophie so angry in all their years here.

"I didn't dissect him. I didn't stick pins through him." Her voice was deadened with fury and suppressed grief. She had never spoken about her previous caretaker. She had never cried at night.

Marie began to smirk, began to open her mouth, and Sophie *moved*. Within moments, she had darted around Heather's body, grabbed the hammer from the floor, and swung it with calculated precision.

She struck Marie in the back of the knee, and the Queen dropped to the floor. She walked around Heather to stand over the Queen. She swung again. And again. And again. Each swing was quicker than Rosalyn could follow; fast, methodical, clinical. Blood bloomed from Marie's knee, her waist, her ribs, her shoulder—it stained the green cotton with blots of red, soaking into the stitching. It coated the ends of the nails that Marie had pushed into the head of the wooden hammer, giving the sceptre its own crown of red. Marie, winded and panting in pain, flung her arm up just in time to catch the next swing that had been about to collide with her head. Having disciplined Marie with her own creation, Queen Sophie reached down and pulled the crown from Marie's grip, flipping it the right way up and setting it on her head.

The new Queen began to drift towards the Throne Room door, placing the Royal Sceptre next to her drawings of the Royal Crest. From downstairs, they heard the *thud* of the front door closing; Matron was back from the village.

"Put the Duchess in gaol for now."

Shaking more than she was willing to admit, Rosalyn crawled to the side of the attic and grabbed one of the big crates that they'd prepared a few weeks ago. Her hands looked almost red in the dusty light. Her palms were stinging. Not wanting to keep Sophie waiting, she dragged the gaol over to Heather and placed it upside-down over her, so that its scribbled label was clear to see. She very carefully didn't look at Marie, on her knees by what used to be her throne.

"If you hurry, you might be able to change clothes and clean yourself up before Matron calls for us, Princess."

Chapter Four – Throne

It was with a sense of relief that Rosalyn gave the back door a good push, stepping outside and letting go so that she wouldn't have to hold it for the others. She took the three steps down quickly, not wanting to waste any time. It was the first day of no rain, and they were allowed outside for exactly one hour. None of the Court had any intention of squandering their time. Marie stepped out right behind her, knocking lighter than she usually would against Rosalyn's left side and moving away, sadly managing to avoid stepping in the particularly muddy patch right in front of Rosalyn, although she did have to circle around it carefully instead of just jumping over it … Rosalyn had been hoping that the other would get a lot of mud on her shoes. That didn't happen, unfortunately, so Rosalyn jumped from the bottom step onto one of the cracked paving stones nearby and then straight to the next one, holding her arms out like she was a bird. The door banged closed behind them, only to be flung open again to make way for Sophie, with Willow and Heather trailing along behind her. Rosalyn found that she couldn't meet Heather's eyes—not that she had tried to—for Heather looked at her feet as soon as Rosalyn glanced in her direction, and Rosalyn refocused on Marie to help squash down the bubbling guilt.

They all watched Marie jump awkwardly along the stepping stones. Matron might have bought Marie's excuse of tripping on the schoolhouse steps, but the Clover Court knew better—her limp was from the Royal Sceptre, held by the Queen.

It was still windy and bitterly cold, so Rosalyn couldn't have her arms stretched out for long, although she'd wanted to fly all the way down to the ditch at the end of the garden. She was sure that one of her hair ribbons was still down there after Marie tossed all her clothing out the dormitory window a month ago. The ribbon would surely be ruined by now, but Rosalyn wanted proof of something else to punish the Princess for. After all, she didn't have long before Marie tried to take the crown back from the Queen, and she couldn't help but relish the feeling of no longer being the most disgraced Princess. Not counting Willow, but that Princess was new and barely qualified as Royalty anyway.

She let her arms drop for just a moment, then lifted them again and soared all the way down the path, jumping over the cracks and gaps in the flagstones as she flew under the grey skies.

"This can be the path to our castle!" It made sense in Rosalyn's mind; the paving stones led all the way up to the back door of the decrepit manor.

"The whole thing can't be the castle! Then Matron and Olivia and Susan would have to be part of it ..." That was Marie, standing stubbornly on a paving stone to avoid the worst of the mud.

Rosalyn had to applaud her audacity, impressed at her decision to speak up against her superiors. She could only guess that the idea of everyone who lived in Hawthorne House becoming a part of their Court was unthinkable enough to Marie that she had to protest beyond silent dissent.

The Clover Court grimaced in unison at that idea—even Willow on the steps. No one wanted Matron or the little kids in the Court.

Rosalyn turned gleefully. "Of course it's not all gonna be the castle," she said with a roll of her eyes, "only the bits that we know belong to the Court, like the Throne Room. Also, this path!"

"But the path is broken." Marie folded her arms as if that would make a bit of difference, sighing as though in exasperation, but Rosalyn was looking directly at her and saw the pain flash across her face as she moved her arm. "It's not fitting for the Court!"

Behind her, Sophie drifted off the bottom step and wandered to the side, past the rickety, rotting shed. With the Queen no longer blocking the way, Rosalyn watched Heather make her way back towards the steps. Rosalyn opened her mouth to retort, but the Queen spoke instead. "So says the lesser Princess ..." She'd walked over to the mossy, crooked wall that ringed the excuse of a garden, and had leaned down as she'd spoken.

Rosalyn frowned and tried to see what was so interesting about the only obstacle between the Court and the sparse, boring fields of Oxfordshire. Honestly, she was kind of glad that the wall reached above their heads; that way, the dreariness that she had to see was limited.

Heather closed the back door with a *snap* and Rosalyn turned to look at her, distracted from her interest in their strange Queen. The older girl had her arms wrapped around her stomach and was determinedly not looking at Sophie or Marie. The dotted ring across her forehead had scabbed over, and her blonde hair was tangled, barely even brushed. How disgraceful for a member of the Clover Court to not look her best! It was Heather's fault for not playing the game properly. It was all Heather's fault. If Rosalyn thought that enough times, it had to be true. Rosalyn hadn't done anything wrong.

Willow reached up as the Duchess went past her to get down the steps, only for her sister to flinch away and lift her hands defensively. Heather picked her way down the last two steps to the ground and went towards the old hawthorn tree that grew right up against the back wall of the manor. The tree might well be dead by now, from how heavily it was creaking in the wind, but Heather didn't seem to care about the chance of a branch falling on her or her shoes scuffing in the muddy grass. She was probably hoping that the Princesses wouldn't want to take that risk. Rosalyn dismissed her with a huff and went back to discreetly watching Sophie. As she did, she caught Heather bending down mechanically and plucking something from the wilting grass in the corner of her eye.

Willow stood up, hugging her storybook to her chest with both arms, and began to hopscotch down the castle path. "I-think-we-should-fetch-the-clovers-now ..." Landing on the stone in front of Marie's, she quickly spun and went back the way she came, the tap-tapping of her shoes ringing out in the chilly garden. "In-case-the-guard-interrupts!"

Rosalyn looked back up at the House. Matron was watching them from a second-floor window with her arms folded, a familiar and disapproving scowl on her face. Probably trying to make sure that there was a full laundry list of things to punish them for, even though she didn't even *try* to understand their game.

"Good idea, Princess." The Queen hadn't responded with her verdict, and so Rosalyn couldn't resist speaking up, taking the opportunity to lord something over Marie. After all, Marie wasn't the Queen anymore, and Rosalyn didn't have to defer to her!

Marie came up behind Willow and with her right arm, pushed her off the path so that she stumbled and nearly slipped, but luckily didn't fall and make her dress dirty.

"We should gather the clovers immediately! Stop standing around and get to work!"

Rosalyn winced, Heather along with her—Marie's voice was loud when she shouted, and shrill, too. Willow glared at the newly fallen Princess but didn't say anything, and Rosalyn giggled to herself. Marie was just grasping at any chance to be more important, and it was so *pitiful* that she couldn't help her laughter. Moving so that one foot was on the next-closest paving stone—there wouldn't be any pushing *her* off the path—Rosalyn started looking for a promising patch of clovers in the scattered clumps of grass.

"The best one wins. Now, choose."

Rosalyn nodded in recognition of Sophie's command and carefully stepped onto the closest patch of grass, making sure to keep her shoes clean of mud.

There was a cluster of clovers growing to her left, and she crouched down and swiftly began plucking as many as she could twist her fingers around. Some mud got under her nails, and she grimaced—she'd pick it out later. The clovers and strands of grass were cold and flimsy against her fingers, holding an almost greyish tint in the lacklustre excuse for sunlight. Clouds papered over the sky as determinedly as the Clover Court battled for Queenship.

"That's enough."

Rosalyn looked over her shoulder to see the Queen standing primly against the mossy wall, clovers in one hand and the slight twist of a smile to her lips. There was no way that she could have gathered them so quickly. Rosalyn realised, too late, that Sophie must have picked them when they had all been distracted by Marie throwing her temper tantrum. Well, that was simply another thing to chalk up against Marie.

Still crouched down, Rosalyn opened her fistful of grass and clovers and sorted through them as quickly as she could. The bits of grass and the obviously damaged clovers went first, followed by all the clovers that didn't have four leaves. That only left two clovers, so she held both of them up and squinted at them. One of them had bigger leaves, so she dropped the failure and went back to the steps, dancing a waltz up the path.

The Court came together at the steps to their castle, each one holding their bounty; a four-leafed clover to show their status in their self-made monarchy. Rosalyn frowned as she looked critically at the clovers that the others had—hers wasn't the biggest *or* the best-looking—those were held by Heather and Sophie, respectively. That wasn't fair! Heather was only a Duchess; Rosalyn thought that it should be the right of a Princess to have a bigger one than those lower than her, but she didn't have the chance to take it before the back door opened.

"All of you, inside. Now. And get that mud off your shoes before you come in. You aren't exempt, Heather." The Court jumped as Matron snapped at them and tucked their clovers into their sleeves before they crossed the threshold to enter their castle. Garden time was over.

※ ※ ※

They didn't have the chance to finish the Royal Charter until sometime before supper, after they had finished their chores for the day. Matron had gone down to the town again to run an errand, and they didn't know how long she would be gone for. Night was falling fast at this time of year, so keeping watch from a window for her return would be difficult.

Not wanting to waste time, Rosalyn ran ahead of the others up the stairs and up into their attic Throne Room, racing to be the one to grab the crown from where it rested. Crown, Charter, and Royal Crest in hand, she left the Throne Room just as the Queen entered.

"Take those downstairs."

"I already am," Rosalyn replied mulishly, forgetting for a moment that being impertinent to *this* Queen was not a good idea.

The look Sophie gave her made her flinch. Rosalyn pretended that her movement had no connection to the way Sophie swung her sceptre up to rest on her shoulder. One of the now-blackened nails was poking at the embroidered collar of her dress. Rosalyn wrenched her gaze away from the hammerhead and hurried back downstairs, making a point to not-quite-run, just in case Sophie was watching her the whole way down. The lower staircase creaked louder than normal as she reached the mid-way steps, but in that moment, all she cared about was that Matron wasn't there to catch them finalising the Charter. They'd wanted to do so in their Throne Room, as was proper, but they wouldn't be able to keep a watch for Matron from there, as the only front-facing window was too dirty to use as a watchtower.

Back in the living room, Sophie sat on the grand armchair by the mantelpiece, while the rest of the Court arranged themselves on the floor around her. Before sitting down in her place by the bookcase, Rosalyn made sure to close the door—that way, if Matron returned early, she wouldn't see them from the main hall. The polished hardwood floorboards were cold against her legs and hard on her knees, but she didn't complain. Just in case. A glance at Marie confirmed that she didn't dare complain either, even though it took her twice as long to sit as it did Rosalyn. When the entire Court was gathered and settled in their places, the Queen finally spoke up.

"This will be the notarisation of the Royal Clover Court official rankings. From this day forth, a Princess who wishes to become Queen must overturn the Queen at least three times, and it must be to the satisfaction of the rest of the Court. A major overturning of the Queen shall equal three minor counts, but must be grand. Additionally, she must overturn each Princess above her. Whomever does so will then take up the Sceptre and wear the Crown. As the Queen has said, so it shall be. The rankings of the monarchy are as follows."

The Queen turned over the piece of paper in her lap, holding it out for the Court to see:

The Royal Clover Court Rankings:

❖ **Queen: Sophie**
❖ *Princess: Rosalyn*
❖ *Princess: Marie*
❖ *Princess: Willow*
❖ *Duchess: Heather*

She waited a few seconds for them to read it, then placed it on the ground at her feet, facing upwards and pointed towards Princess Marie. Rosalyn, sitting opposite, tried to read it again.

"Understood?"

"Yes, Queen." They answered together, their voices not quite meshing into one.

"But Rosalyn's not—"

"She currently outranks you, Princess Marie. Understood?"

Marie folded her arms and glared at Rosalyn. Rosalyn made sure to smile sweetly and stare right back at her.

"Understood?" The Queen reached down to take hold of her sceptre, and Princess Marie flinched.

A moment when Rosalyn tried to brace herself.

And Marie broke. "Fine."

Queen Sophie let go of her sceptre and turned her black gaze on Duchess Heather, who bit at her lip and looked away.

"There is a red candle underneath that drape. Bring it here."

The Duchess didn't move until the Queen pointed at the drape in question, at which point she scrambled to her feet and walked over with slow, shaky steps. Princess Marie laughed none-too-quietly, and Rosalyn hid a smile behind her hand—it *was* sort of funny.

The small red candle was still there, to Rosalyn's relief, and she watched as Heather knelt to tug it out from under the heavy curtain. The cuff of her sleeve was covered in dust when she turned back around and crawled back over to the Court, taking her place again to Rosalyn's left and setting the candle down on the floor.

"Princess Willow, the clovers."

Willow leaned forwards to drop the handful of clovers onto the Charter, then sat back on her heels. The clovers would form part of the wax seal that would make the Charter official; one clover per Royal.

Queen Sophie pulled a match out from her sleeve and made to rise, but Rosalyn spoke up before she could lower herself down to the floor, not wanting to lose the best chance she'd had in weeks to get back at Marie. Queen Sophie and Marie had spent the entire time underestimating her, thinking that she was a lesser Princess, barely above a Duchess. Rosalyn wanted to be Queen, and she knew something that Princess Willow and Duchess Heather didn't, something that the current Queen had no need to use yet. But Rosalyn *did*.

"Shouldn't Princess Marie do it? Menial work is below us, right?"

The Queen was silent in apparent thought for a moment before she reached out and dropped the match in front of Princess Marie, who stared at it in poorly concealed disbelief.

"What's the matter, *Princess*? Scared of a little old match?" Willow finally spoke up, her tone filled with taunting, jeering hate. To Rosalyn's ears, she barely sounded like the gentle and shy girl who'd shown up on the doorstep two weeks ago, hollowed-out inside.

"I'm not scared, Princess!" Marie snatched the match from the floor and grabbed the candle, then got up and walked to the cabinet next to the window, her left leg dragging slightly. The Princess opened the cabinet and took the box of matches off the top shelf, striking the Court's match against it quickly. The flame blossomed, and Marie swallowed hard, holding the match to the candle wick until it caught light. As soon as the wick flared up, Princess Marie blew out the match and dropped it onto the floor. She walked triumphantly back over to the assembled Court, stooping down to place the candle on the corner of the Charter.

Princess Marie kneeled down, and her sleeve shifted as she extended her arm. The Court watched as the Princess looked down. The Court watched as the lace trim leaned into the flame. The Court watched as the frozen Princess stiffened into statue, stone-still in terror, mouth stuck shut.

Princess Rosalyn realised, too late, what was happening, and began to throw herself away from the Charter and the candle and the Princess, the Princess who dropped the candle. The Princess who stared in open, trembling terror, but didn't react as the flames licked up her sleeve and fell down into her lap as the cotton and the lace burned away and—and the candle landed on its side and rolled across the Charter, which caught and began to burn and curl up around the pooling drops of molten wax—

And the Queen was rising, the Clover Court was moving, but Rosalyn didn't see much more than that. Not looking back, she stumbled to her feet and ran for the door, the door that she'd shut, the door that she wasted a few valuable seconds to pull open. The others must be saying something—Princess Marie must surely be screaming as she burned—but Rosalyn heard nothing except for the ringing in her ears that sounded like the school's fire bell.

And then she was in the main hall, running and stumbling and fleeing towards the dining room. Through the double doors. Into the lifeless, freezing-cold kitchen.

There were no buckets, the buckets were upstairs, and Rosalyn spun around in frantic desperation, looking for something, anything. There was nothing she could use. She had to do something.

With nothing else at hand, she turned the tap on with a wrench of the handle and shoved the plug into the drain before she ran from the kitchen and out through the dining room and into the main hall. She could smell the smoke now; it was billowing out of the living-room door and filling the hall. Her hands were wet, but that hardly mattered.

And Duchess Heather was stumbling through the smoke towards the locked front door, her skirt and sleeves and hair on fire, and her mouth was open and she might be crying and she might be screaming, but Rosalyn heard no sound.

The fire was spilling out into the main hall and crawling up the walls like spiders climbing webs to catch a caught moth. Crowding up against the ceiling, the smoke gathered and hung like storm clouds, only thickening when the fire latched onto the ceiling and reached the first floor. A staggering, limp-limbed movement caught her eye, and Rosalyn looked back down across the entrance hall as Duchess Heather fell to the floor like a ragdoll, and Rosalyn felt her head begin to shake from side to side to side to side.

She ran for the first floor, feeling the steps begin to give way under her feet as she threw herself up them. There was something behind her, and she glanced back to see Princess Willow at her heels and the main hall burning, flames reaching up like claws to grab and rip and tear at the staircase.

A figure in dark blue whirled through the fire from the dining room doors and around towards the staircase; Matron had locked the front door, and the back door must also be locked for the Queen to still be in the building. There was no way out. The flames leaped to the staircase and started eating it hungrily, spreading up the bannisters and rushing onto the steps proper as the Queen ascended, and Rosalyn couldn't look back anymore.

Princess Rosalyn reached the first-floor landing with a choking gasp and went to run to the closest cupboard, the one filled with spiders that Matron had put the cleaning supplies in after the Court wouldn't stop trapping the little kids under the buckets. She didn't get that far.

The floor shook under Rosalyn's feet, and she felt, more than saw, the huge, ancient staircase crash down to the ground floor with a geyser of sparks and burning chips of wood, tearing away from the first-floor landing. She turned around even though she didn't want to.

She *had* to, and so she did.

There was no staircase left. No staircase. No Queen. Only smoke and smouldering sticks of wood. The fire on the ground floor surged higher, fiercer, stronger from the new fuel that burned so easily.

Sparks fizzled on the old, dry floorboards and burst into greedy, starving flames, spilling across the landing like a flood. Princess Rosalyn reeled backwards, falling against the cupboard and not even caring as thousands of Sophie's spiders scattered over her and up the wall, trying to get away.

Willow should've been right there, she'd been just behind her only a few moments ago, and Rosalyn looked about in confusion even as she pushed away from the spider cupboard. The smoke was coming thick and fast, sparks spitting up still, and it took far too long for Rosalyn to find Princess Willow again.

She was at the edge of the landing, right where the stairs had met with the first floor, and she was about to fall.

No words came out of her mouth, even though her lips were moving, and Rosalyn could only stare at her panic-stricken, anguished face as the Princess clawed at the rotted, collapsing, burning floorboards. Rosalyn felt herself moving backwards into the hallway, watching as the Princess became silhouetted against the flames around her.

This is all your fault, Ros-a-lyn!

And Princess Willow vanished as the landing was engulfed in flame.

Princess Rosalyn ran for the dormitories, knowing that the window in between Marie's and Sophie's beds was the only one that could be opened; Marie had thrown all her clothes from there once upon a time.

The first floor was burning, the first floor was burning and she could barely see for the smoke. It was all she could do to hopscotch around the flames that grasped at her shoes and skirt and stockings.

Left.

Forwards.

Right.

Forwards.

Down the hall.

The smoke was much thicker here, and the door opposite the Clover Court's dormitory was open. Little Olivia had collapsed on the smouldering floor just beyond the doorway, utterly still. Behind her was Susan, doll-like. Face down.

Choking on ash and horrified terror, she shouldered open her dormitory door and ran for Sophie's bed, directly opposite her. The floor in here was bending and warping under her every step; smoke was streaming up through the floorboards, accompanied by sparks. It should have been creaking, but she couldn't tell. Princess Rosalyn scrambled up onto the Queen's bed and reached up to grab at the rusted handle to the window.

It broke off in her hand with a *snap*.

Rosalyn stared at the remnant in her grip. She couldn't open the window at all. The handle slipped from her betrayal-numbed fingers. This was the only window in the dormitory that could be opened. She pushed against the glass pane as hard as she could. Nothing.

She hit with her fist as hard as she could. It didn't move.

Third time wasn't so lucky after all.

The floor began to burn.

There was a dead moth on the windowsill. Black, like soot.

Dead moths. Dead butterflies. Dead spiders. The jar.

Rosalyn could see it now; Queen Sophie had hidden it well, but not well enough. She reached down to grab the neck of the jar and lifted it high, then held it in both hands and swung it as hard as she could at the window. But her hands were wet, they'd gotten wet in the kitchen, and the jar tumbled from her hands. She crouched down to try to find it again, but she couldn't see through the smoke and the lashes of flame. The floor was starting to give way, and still, still, all Princess Rosalyn could hear was the school fire bell.

The bed began tilting under her and she stood as the dormitory began to shake, and she reached to grasp onto the partially crumbled windowsill.

The floor fell away with a great rending of wood and red-orange flame, folding like crumpled paper, down into what had been the kitchen. Sparks and crowds of black specks gushed up where the floor and the beds had just been—soot settled in her lashes and hair, making it hard to see. If she blinked, her eyes would get stuck shut. Princess Rosalyn clung on and tried to pull herself up onto the narrow windowsill. If she could just get high enough, maybe, maybe—

She failed. Her fingers slipped a little. Ash was gathering under her nails, and it felt like they were starting to lift away from the strain.

With nowhere to go except through the window that might as well be a mile away, Rosalyn didn't dare look down at the inferno that swirled below her, consuming Hawthorne House ravenously. She wondered where her crown had gone. Maybe Queen Sophie still had it. Princess Rosalyn wanted to wear it, just once. She wanted to be the Queen. She'd only wanted to be the Queen, just once. She never got to wear the crown legitimately. Hadn't she done enough to earn it?

Acrid smoke filled her mouth and throat and she coughed. Again and again, she coughed.

Princess Willow had been right; this *was* all her fault. Her fault for complaining of boredom to the others. Her fault for coming up with The Clover Court so long ago. Her fault for playing when Duchess Heather told them to stop. Her fault for making Princess Marie light the candle. Her fault.

Ash coated her tongue, cloying and choking her. She gasped in another breath, but nothing reached her lungs. It was beginning to rain again. Too late to help. She saw the raindrops splattering against the window and trickling down, ten inches from her face but so far away. Her fingers were slipping more and more and more. The flames were at her shoes now, licking at her ankles. It hurt. It hurt so much. Her fault.

And
Princess
Rosalyn
Let
Go.

Part Two – Delicate Negotiations

Chapter One – Do Not Disturb

(July 1939)

Andrew Endley opened his eyes and let go of the circlet of barbed wire in his hands, coughing on the taste of ash and smoke, crayons and clovers. His hands felt like they were burning, his fingertips stinging in pain; the metal crown looked almost red-hot for the moment it took for him to adjust to where he was. He was in the remains of Hawthorne House. He was standing in the area that the floorplan said was the living room. He wasn't falling, wasn't burning, wasn't …

He didn't know how long he'd been standing there. His head was pounding, and his breath came fast and heavy; he lifted a hand to rub at his eyes and found his skin to be covered in a thin layer of ash. He wiped it off on his shirt quickly, trying to pretend that he wasn't trembling.

"Do you see, now?"

He lifted his gaze to see someone he'd only glimpsed in the backs of spoons, looking both down yet up at him from puddles and, in her last moments, staring in terror from the reflection of a rain-struck window.

Rosalyn.

The rumour was that the orphanage had burned down out of nowhere, and that all seven of the children living there had perished in the blaze; the Matron had been out on an errand of some kind, only to return too late to save anyone. It was whispered that the sound of children playing could be heard in the remains, and trespassers would be lucky to only find their pockets filled with dead insects, broken crayons, or limp four-leafed clovers. That something tangible remained of the deceased children.

He tore his eyes away from her to look down again at the crown, understanding now. "I ... well ..." What could he say? What could he possibly say to the nine-year-old girl that he could sort of see if he stopped pretending otherwise, standing in front of him and staring sadly, a flickering circle of barbed wire upon her head? "Thank you for sharing with me what happened, Rosalyn. *Princess* Rosalyn."

In the space of a blink, the translucent little girl was gone, and he was left staring open-mouthed at the patch of rubble between the crown and the bare-brick wall, the death-faded purple of her dress still inked in his vision. He took a moment to try to compose himself, then he carefully lifted the crown and moved it out of the way so no one would step on it, making sure to hold it between the barbs. The barbed wire was just as cold as it had been when he'd initially picked it up, and to his intense relief, no more memories came to wash him away.

With nothing remaining of the upper floors and the manor a slowly crumbling shell, the rest of the Evacuation Volunteer Brigade were still sorting through the twisted remains of what had once been the kitchen of Hawthorne House. Time had rusted the surviving metal black, and ivy had tangled itself around whatever plumbing remained. He had to make sure to tell the group not to remove the barbed-wire crown, nor any other items found, from the manor. Doing so wouldn't be wise, considering their significance to the 'Clover Court'. If Rosalyn remained, he thought it likely that the rest of the children did as well. The local townspeople avoided the ruins of the orphanage, claiming the place to have been cursed for the thirteen years since the fire. Their conviction of the site's haunted status was pervasive enough to be recorded in his documents on the manor; Andrew had known to expect whispers, perhaps a hint of a presence or occasional oddities. Not a full apparition. And he highly doubted that only Rosalyn had remained.

He would have to be careful not to disturb them, especially so once Hawthorne House had been rebuilt. After all, the shell of the manor was still intact, the foundations were solid, and the building plan was sound; Hawthorne House would be useful in the war effort once it had been cleaned up and rebuilt, filled with ghosts or not. As the project manager of sorts, ensuring everything went as smoothly as possible would be Andrew's job. The intention was to restore the building to as close to the state it had been in before the fire, though more structurally sound, down to the layout and purpose of each room. Doing so would provide lodgings for at least ten children, allowing the number of evacuees to the town to be a little higher.

The ten-minute cycle back to his bed-and-breakfast was more of a blur than a journey, driven by the rushing thoughts in his head more so than the wind helping to push his bicycle down the hill. He stopped only long enough to ensure that his bicycle leant securely against the wall, and walked briskly into his temporary accommodation, nodding to his hostess in the foyer. The hostess said something to him as he rushed past, but replying cordially was the last thing on his mind: he had notes to make before the details of his interaction with Rosalyn faded any further.

Andrew took the stairs two at a time, grabbing onto the bannister as his knee twinged painfully—he was *much* too old for playing pretend games with his niece, that was certain (she'd asked, as he'd been about to travel here for his work, and who was he to refuse?). His room was much as he'd left it; slightly larger than a box room, with an untouched bed, a functional desk, and a small washbasin in the corner. The curtains, however, had been pushed back, and a thick quilt left folded at the end of the bed—presumably to help ward off the chilly nights here. The maid had obviously come in whilst he had been up at the ruined manor. His satchel was still on the desk where he'd left it, and he made a beeline for both.

Thankfully, the provided chair wasn't too uncomfortable, and he rubbed at his knee as he retrieved first his notebook, and then the case folder for Hawthorne House. Withdrawing the collated information on supernatural activity found the section given over to the ghostly presences severely lacking in detail; the first thing he did was update *'suspected residual presence: deceased orphans'* to *'confirmed full corporeal apparition: deceased orphan 'Rosalyn', 9 yrs; suspected full corporeal apparition: deceased orphans (x six maximum)'*. Luckily, his past self had possessed enough foresight to leave plenty of space for additional notes; even so, he added several sheafs of paper to the file, and began to write all that he could recall.

Of greatest importance was the confirmation that Rosalyn's spirit persisted, as well as his experience with accidentally touching a trigger object—the barbed-wire 'crown'. Such an object could retain a spirit's emotion, but to throw him into a spirit's *memories* of life ... His hand was shaking a little, so he laid down his pen and took a moment.

He had to go about this rationally; allowing himself to be overcome with fear would help no one: not the spirits, not the imminent workmen, not future evacuees, and certainly not himself. Even so, his chest ached, and his fingers shook too badly to hope to hold a pen steady.

Standing abruptly, he pushed his chair back from the desk and strode several times around the room, fighting the urge to yell in delayed fright, or perhaps vomit. He'd had some dealings with full apparitions before, and many more with residual spirits, but all of those with any retained personality had been adults. Usually desiring one specific thing, be it closure or revenge—but these were *children*. These were children who'd died because of a horrible, malicious, *stupid* game. Their unfinished business couldn't be as simple as seeing the house rebuilt—their goal had been to win the game, above all else—and something unidentifiable welled in him at the realisation that they'd likely never be able to pass on. If they even wanted to. They'd be stuck in their game infinitely, and he wondered if they knew that. He wondered if they even cared.

One couldn't see the manor house (or the hill it sat on) from the inn he was lodging in, but he found himself glancing in its general direction anyway, speculating on what Rosalyn and the other children (in their likely, regrettable existence) could be doing at that moment. Probably playing that dreadful game, still. As in life, the game continued to dominate their world. His breath came short at the thought as he started to ruminate on what, exactly, they could be plotting, and he turned abruptly to face the opposite direction.

Think about something else.

He ran a hand through his hair, winced as a cuticle caught on a strand, and took a deep breath. He took another, and the clenching in his chest began to ease. The spirits had been confirmed to exist, yes. The fact that not only Rosalyn, but likely at least four other children, were forced to remain in the miserable house where they'd died was terrible. However, Rosalyn hadn't been hostile to him. He could work with her, and any other spirits remaining at the site. He'd taken this job knowing that there was practically confirmed spirit activity; backing out now was hardly an option. He just—

He just had to play their game.

Play along.

Although, their 'Clover Court' game was extremely dangerous, and apparitions of the strength that Rosalyn had demonstrated would potentially be able to impact the living, if they tried hard enough ... If he was to avoid drawing their ire, he couldn't try to insert himself into their delicate hierarchy; nor did the idea appeal to him. He tried to approach the situation how his niece would, and that helped to settle his mind some.

The children were playing a game of monarchies ... Perhaps he could take on the role of an ambassador from a different 'kingdom'? Doing so would allow him to talk to the spirits with civility, and their own rules would hopefully prevent them from trying to hurt him. He wouldn't be a member of their 'Court', after all.

He wouldn't be a member of their Court; if they were to accept him into their game, allowing him to interact with them, he would be much safer than if they viewed him as they did their old Matron. Andrew suspected the ghosts of the orphans would turn on him if they thought that he was trying to control them. They certainly wouldn't be scared of him, not like they were of their old Matron. *However*, if they saw him as someone who was also playing their game, someone who had a role with authority, though not part of their 'monarchy'... his safety was much more certain.

He could do this.

Not only could he do this, he knew that he was the best candidate for the job: he wasn't frightened of ghosts, per se. Furthermore, he had come up with a way to interact hopefully ... peacefully with the spirits, and he was prepared to go through with it.

He could do this.

The frantic seizing in his chest and throat seemed to have calmed—he took another deep breath and rolled his shoulders carefully, then shook out his hands and retook his seat at the desk. He had important notes to write, after all, and was relieved to find that his pen no longer trembled when he lifted it to the page. He would have to prepare himself each time he sought out Rosalyn or her compatriots; fear would be useful if he wanted to flee the manor, not to have a conversation with the ghostly inhabitants.

Before he forgot, he scribed as many of Rosalyn's memories as he could easily recall—the game she'd invented, the arrival of the Phillips sisters, the confrontation in the attic (the violence and the blood it brought; the crown *pushing into the blonde girl's head*, the *hammer*). The girl named Marie dropping the candle. The fire. The memory of the fire and the events directly preceding it were clearer in his mind than the rest—because for a moment, he'd felt like *he* was the one burning instead of poor Rosalyn, his brain 'helpfully' supplied—and thus, he could still recall the rules from when the taciturn Sophie had spoken them.

'*It was a game of one-uppance*', he wrote, '*wherein each player must play a trick or prank, often cruel, on the players higher in rank*'. He tapped his pen to his lips, trying to articulate the rest; Sophie's recital had been for show, assuming that everyone listening knew the game. '*The aim of their game was to become 'Queen', and lord authority over the other players. The game was a make-believe one of a royal court; the setting informed how they acted around one another, to an extent. They were aware the 'royal' aspect of the game was pretend, but did not care.*'

He turned the page and began to form a rough timeline of events, unfortunately sans dates; Rosalyn's memories hadn't included a long look at a calendar or a written down date, but he supposed the exact timings of the various incidents didn't matter in the long run. What mattered was that they had happened and had likely induced a lasting effect. Of particular note was Rosalyn making the 'crown', the arrival of the Phillips sisters, the lavatory incident with the locket, the twofold attack in the attic, and lastly, the cause of the fire itself; Rosalyn's coercion of Marie.

With as much of their game detailed that he could recall, Andrew went to the next page and made sure to note down any other potential trigger objects at Hawthorne House besides the 'crown': he thought the hammer with the nails in the head was likely, given how it had been used in the attic, as well as Sophie's jar of bugs—not only had it seemed to be Sophie's most prized possession, it had also failed to break the window during Rosalyn's attempt at escaping the fire. The locket that Rosalyn had found in the toilet and thusly been accused of planting there also made the list, and, upon wracking his memory for anything the late elder sister might have maintained enough of an attachment to for such a strong connection to be made—Aha! The brooch that Rosalyn had seen pinned under the girl's mattress would probably suffice as an anchor.

He wasn't so naive to think that rebuilding Hawthorne House would allow them to move on, but hopefully, he'd be able to convince them of the benefits of a rebuild. After all, the burning down of the mansion had been unintentional, as far as he could remember.

Chapter Two – Play a Game

(October 1939)

It was some months later when he returned to the building site, now significantly more than just a shell of a once-grand manor house. The men were packing up to leave for the day; night was falling fast, hurried along by November's approach. He made sure to give them all a friendly nod as they passed, waving off the concern of some of the more perceptive builders. He didn't blame them for their worries over him, especially considering how there had been a few reports of strange activity at Hawthorne House: materials going missing and important measurements in the plans being found scribbled over in crayon, for the most part. Andrew needed to convince the ghostly inhabitants to stop trying to sabotage the building work, although he was well aware that they could be doing far worse—none of the builders had been attacked, thankfully, but Andrew didn't want to rely on their apparent reluctance to hurt an adult. It would be foolish to make the assumption that would last. Of highest priority was the roof; the reconstruction was behind schedule due to spirit-induced delays, and so the builders had been forced to bring forward the completion of some form of roof; the building had to be watertight before winter arrived at their doorstep.

That was the reason for this particular visit: he wished to make contact with Rosalyn again and figure out why either she or what he presumed to be the ghosts of the other children were going out of their way to make things difficult for the builders. Surely, the spirits would have realised that the workers were there to rebuild Hawthorne House; they *had* to have noticed the transformation from a burnt-out, overgrown shell to a barely habitable building. Andrew hoped their resistance was due to disliking adults accidentally interfering with their game or interrupting them with construction noise, rather than a desire to see Hawthorne House remain a ruin. With luck, he would be able to convince them to stop, but he had the sinking suspicion, all but confirmed, that he would only have a chance as long as he played along with their 'Clover Court' game and at least gave the appearance of genuinely desiring to be a part of it—the last thing he wanted was for the spirits to turn on him. In retrospect, he really should have instigated this conversation with the ghosts before building work had started, but with all the meetings he'd had to have with the local council, he had wrongly assumed that it would be fine to leave a little late. Hindsight was very valuable; hopefully Rosalyn and the others wouldn't hold it against him.

He'd chosen a weekday to make the fifteen-minute cycle up the hill and was somewhat regretting his choice to leave his jacket behind; whilst travelling to the build site had kept him warm enough, it was much windier up on the hill than down in the town. They were firmly in autumn now—colder weather was fast approaching. Aware of rain's imminent arrival, he already missed the sporadic sun of summer ... he really should have brought his jacket.

The clouds were thick enough that the setting sun had softened into a dull yellow, and he refocused on the interior of the manor, stepping through the temporary frame of the front doorway. Although generally left tidy, he still took care as he crossed the threshold—tripping over a stray beam or toolbox would be *most* unwelcome.

The dim, somewhat musty foyer greeted him, utterly silent. The downstairs hadn't been worked on for a few days, due to the rush to reconstruct the roof; the work of laying the baseboards had stopped midway across the ground floor. Sawdust and the occasional metal shaving dusted the unfinished floor. He glanced around as he entered—Rosalyn was nowhere to be seen, nor could he spy any signs of her 'friends'. That was probably for the best, at least whilst he got his bearings; even with just the interior walls hastily constructed, standing in a building that was starting to resemble the one from Rosalyn's memories was more jarring than he had anticipated. Everything seemed a little lower, the spaces for the windows looking wrong until he realised—of *course*—he was remembering the house from the height of a nine-year-old. He took a deep breath to prepare himself, glad that he wasn't asthmatic, and went to look for the 'Clover Court'.

He'd spent some spare hours over the last several months researching the children who'd once lived here, supplementing the rather pitiful surviving records with anecdotes wheedled out of the few townies willing to talk to him about the ruined manor house. He wished he'd thought to bring his notes on Rosalyn and her peers, but they remained in the drawer of the desk lent to him.

He had planned to go into the living room space first because that was where he'd met Rosalyn. As he headed in that direction, however, an odd sound to his right distracted him. A faint, almost-scraping sound. The living room was to his left, thus the noise couldn't be coming from there. Under other circumstances, he would have turned around and left, but regretfully, he knew that he'd likely have to interrupt whomever was currently manifesting in the right-hand side of the house. He dearly hoped they wouldn't be too angry with him, or he could find himself in serious danger.

He walked towards the sound, placing his feet so as to make as little noise as possible. That terrible clenching in his chest was making itself known to him again, but turning around would negate the whole point of taking this job. He just had to remain calm. If this were Rosalyn, he liked to think that she would have made herself known in some way. He nearly called out but caught the words as they rose in his throat—whoever or whatever it may be might not take kindly to sudden noises. Something crunched and cracked under his shoe, and he glanced down to find a piece of chalk, broken and crushed into the floor.

Remain calm.

The scratching paused for a moment, then continued, and now that he was closer, he could hear indistinct muttering under the noise of the chalk. Bracing himself and trying to remember as much as he could of the Clover Court and its members, Andrew rounded the doorway into what would be the dining room.

At first, he thought the room was empty and he'd been mistaken, but then he saw them; the barely there sketches of two figures huddled under one of the tall windows at the back of the building, taking turns to lean over the paper on the floor between them and bring their heads together. The setting sun only allowed a faint outline to be seen, but eventually, the two became a little clearer to his sight, until he could even see suggestions of colour in their clothes and hair. Like Rosalyn, they didn't look like they'd burned to death, but their translucency unnerved him enough to halt him in his tracks.

The pair either hadn't noticed him or simply didn't care much for his presence; the little girl on the left in the brown dress and long hair in plaits down her back—*Willow, this was Willow*, the one who'd fallen from the landing—lifted her hand to hide a whisper to the taller, blonde girl, who bent her head to listen before nodding vigorously, and both shook with silent giggles. For an instant, all he could see was the blonde girl crumpling to the floor, burning, before the moment passed and he managed to refocus on Heather and her sister. Their backs to him, they probably hadn't intended to show themselves just yet. Andrew didn't know for certain if the children were still playing their game as devoutly as they had whilst alive, but he wouldn't be terribly surprised if the sisters were plotting against the other girls, or perhaps coming up with new ideas for their 'castle'. He hoped for the latter, given how the battle for the role of 'Queen' had played out in the weeks before the fire … At least he could hopefully take solace in their probable inability to cause significant harm to one another. A small comfort, but from their reaction in the attic to Heather standing up for herself, he was glad that their interactions with the living seemed to be limited; else he was certain that they would have driven the builders away by now for the 'crime' of interrupting them.

The wind blew louder, rushing through the gaps where the windows would go and ruffling his shirt; he drew his arms around himself to try to hold off the chill. The pair of spirits didn't seem affected.

As he pondered his situation, shifting from one foot to the other, a piece of chalk fell from his trouser pocket and clattered to the floor. It had not been there before. He jumped, but not as hard as the Phillips sisters. Two faces jerked around to stare at him, skinny shoulders half-turned, one sister's eyes narrowed in suspicion, the other's startled, shocked. Andrew barely had time to take a breath, his hands flying up to reassure them, and then the pair were gone. Not a trace of them left, aside from the chalk and paper left lying on the floor under the window. He blinked and swallowed hard, rubbing at his eyes and trying to scrub away the afterimage of their two faces, but particularly Heather's, dark blood dripping into her wide eyes from the oozing puncture marks across her forehead.

He began to walk towards the abandoned paper, but he'd barely moved when he heard the unmistakable sound of footsteps on floorboards somewhere above him—several sets of shoes.

There were no floorboards on the first floor.

The whole floor had to be navigated via planks placed between support beams. He doubted this was his imagination playing tricks on him, and although it could simply be paranoia, he found himself reluctant to consider it such; the incident with Rosalyn combined with the fresh encounter stood stark in his mind. From where he was in the incomplete dining room, the papers looked mostly unmarked, and so he made a mental note to return here later for a closer examination before turning to walk back into the entrance hall. He could still hear pacing above him, as though someone were walking toe-to-toe in a figure of eight, over and over again.

There was something behind him.

In the split second after he realised, he felt the sort of lurch that came in the moments just before something terrible happened, and he ducked in the doorway, lifting his arms to cover his head.

The metal tin thudded against the wooden doorpost and split open along the seam, scores of nails showering down onto him and scattering every which way. Nails hit against his arms and shoulders and fell to the ground; he jerked upright and spun to look behind him whilst the nails rolled in lazy circles on the unfinished floor. If he hadn't ducked, it would have hit his head.

"What the—" His exclamation caught in his throat. Marie was standing two metres away from him, arms folded, her expression twisted into an unhappy frown. It *had* to be Marie; he couldn't help but recognise her. Just like the three he'd seen already, so, too, was her outline traced in the empty space, a subtle distortion of the air that grew clearer the longer he stared at it. From the wounds upon Heather, he half-expected to see this girl's dress to be splotched with blood or wreathed in flames; thankfully, there were no visual reminders of what had happened in the attic or the fire.

She'd just attempted to hit him on the head with a tin full of nails. He took a step backwards, frantically trying to think of something to say that wouldn't provoke her any further. If he was being honest with himself, Marie concerned him the most of the deceased children; she was violent in a way that Rosalyn, Willow, and Heather simply weren't, and had a much shorter fuse than Sophie. Undoubtedly, whatever reason she disliked him for had been decided on the spot, and he simply didn't know if trying to dissuade her would only make her angrier with him. In the back of his mind, he made note of her appearance to add later to his document on the ghosts here. His interruption of Heather and Willow Phillips had been an accident, yet Marie had sought him out deliberately, even throwing a tin of nails at him …

The ghost took a silent step forward. She was glaring at him, and his heart jumped into his mouth at the malice in her eyes.

He was about to ask why she had attacked him, and to ask what he could do to fix it, but had to change tack quickly—the little girl was reaching down for a pair of pliers that lay near her shoe.

"Wait—don't! I just want to have a word with you, with the Clover Court. It's very important."

Marie paused, then straightened up, her expression smoothing from hostility to puzzled curiosity. Internally, Andrew rejoiced at actually getting somewhere with his intention to talk to the children, with a bonus of distracting her from those pliers.

Her mouth moved, but he could hear nothing. At his lack of comprehension, she blinked and promptly vanished, leaving him to gape at the space she had just occupied. Not half a second later, she reappeared in the same place, her arms folded again. Her gaze still burned into him, but suspicion seemed to have replaced rage. Andrew thanked small mercies for that.

"Mr Andrew Endley! You came back!"

He half-turned to his right. Rosalyn was taking a few quick steps forward, colour and substance blooming into being as he watched. Marie shifted away as she approached, studiously ignoring the pliers that until ten seconds ago, she'd been prepared to throw at him. From what he'd gleaned of the past, she wasn't the type to retreat from something, unless ... He glanced back at Rosalyn—the barbed-wire crown was set on her head.

He was certain of it now: in the aftermath of the fire, Rosalyn had become the Queen of that infernal game. It made a horrific sort of sense, he supposed, because it had been *her* idea to make Marie light the candle, meaning that the blame for the fire could be placed squarely on Rosalyn. He was reasonably sure that her urging for Marie to handle the match had been an act of revenge combined with a bid for the crown, given Rosalyn's knowledge of Marie's history of surviving a house fire and subsequent pyrophobia. Although, he hoped that she couldn't have wanted to do more than perhaps entice the wrath of the Court at Marie for ruining the Charter. But she had made the deliberate decision to push the role of melting the wax to Marie, taking credit in the eyes of the Court for what would happen next. The resulting fire had directly stemmed from Rosalyn's choice, and the crown she now wore showed the judgement bestowed by her subjects. The ultimate one-uppance to hold over the other children: the responsibility for their deaths, if unintentional. The posthumous Queen of the Clover Court.

He cleared his throat, a little self-consciously, and hoped that he was about to make the right decision. "Ah, yes. I hoped to speak to you again, as well as the Royal Clover Court in full. Could—"

"We can't start yet, not until everyone's here. My Court, my rules." Gone was the brief excitement and pleasant demeanour she'd shown upon realising he was there; *this* Rosalyn spoke firmly, watching him unblinkingly. He'd thought he'd come to know Rosalyn—as much as one could through reliving their memories—but the stark realisation that he'd never known her as the *Queen* crept through him like a sudden chill.

This Rosalyn was not a friend.

He nodded and carefully leaned against the doorpost to wait, rather uncomfortable under the weight of the two girls' gaze. Surreptitiously, he took a deep breath, and then another, trying to push his fear down instead of letting it show. His finger tapped uncontrollably against his leg, so he shoved his hand into his trouser pocket to hide it. He shouldn't be scared of them—they were only children— but he couldn't help but remember the hammer, the crown, the fire; they were dead, and had been for over a decade. *They'd been dead for longer than they'd lived.* He couldn't just wait in silence, and so he opened his mouth to speak again, raising a hand placatingly at the twin glares—this wasn't for the Court.

"Miss Rosalyn—*Queen* Rosalyn."

Something shifted in how she stood, seeming slightly friendlier, and she didn't stop him.

"Thank you for hearing me out. I hope you will trust me with the manor, and thank you for letting me touch the crown." He'd been about to say more, but his voice failed as the feeling of eyes on him increased tenfold, analysing and dissecting everything about him. He couldn't breathe. It wasn't safe here. It wasn't safe, he was surrounded by ghosts, the walls could collapse in at any moment, they would wrap him in barbed wire and use it to rip his face off if he said the wrong thing—

No, the walls were sound, he'd checked. He knew how to play pretend from his nieces; he'd be just fine. He wasn't considered part of their Court; they wouldn't dare to attack him like they might a fellow 'Royal'...

He took a breath, looking around, just to reaffirm his thoughts. Heather was sitting on a workbench on the other side of Rosalyn, her arms folded as she glared at him, and as soon as he realised that Heather was present, he felt the crushing fear begin to lessen. Ah. The fear—at least in part—had originated from Heather. The claustrophobia element to it, he suspected. He couldn't stop staring at the dripping blood. "Ah—"

"You may speak now, Mr Endley. This meeting of the Clover Court with a visiting Ambassador is now in session."

Heather and Willow were inseparable, and he didn't think that Rosalyn would exclude Sophie on purpose, out of fear of retribution; therefore, Willow and Sophie must also be present, even if he couldn't see them. That feeling of being examined was still present; he was starting to believe the unsettling, unrelenting observation came from Sophie. It was Sophie. Not being able to see her didn't sit well with him.

He frowned for a moment, unsure where to start, then cleared his throat and began to speak, the notion of treading carefully and watching his words hammering a mantra in his mind. In addition to apologising for any upset he or the workers may have caused, he needed to convince them not to interfere in the rebuilding of Hawthorne House, as well as ensure that he was on good terms with the girls ... Delicate negotiations, indeed.

He could do this. He just had to find the words. The girls—the ones that he could perceive, anyway—watched him with unblinking intensity.

"Thank you for hearing me. I come to the Royal Clover Court with a proposal I hope will be found acceptable. This proposal is the rebuilding of the castle to its original form, though much improved structurally, and furnished anew." Andrew took a breath and folded his hands in front of him. They hadn't stopped him yet, and the lump of terror sitting somewhere in his sternum hadn't worsened, and so he continued. "In addition, I would like to become the official Ambassador between the Clover Court and anyone outside, acting as liaison should any issues arise."

That brought a significant reaction from the spirits; Queen Rosalyn tilted her head, lifting a hand to her chin in apparent thought, and Sophie's form traced itself into existence, sitting on the wall where a window would fit. Something moved on her buckled shoe, and he watched a spider emerge from the leather, crawl to the underside on spindly legs, and detach from the sole.

"I am aware of the rules that the Clover Court abides by, and whilst I would like to play, I do not believe myself worthy of a Royal position; an Ambassadorial role is all I wish for." He'd presented the most pressing points—the manor's restoration, his potential role as a liaison, and his deferral from participating in the Court proper—not wanting to speak past his welcome, he bowed his head briefly, moving his hands back to his sides to indicate that he was done. After a moment to steady himself, he looked back up to analyse their reactions.

The Clover Court seemed to be thrown for a loop, almost; Heather leaned a little to the side, as though listening to someone, presumably Willow, and Rosalyn, Marie, and Sophie shared a glance.

The first to speak was Rosalyn, measured and even. "The rebuilding of our castle would be welcomed." Her tone turned thoughtful, considering the rest of the proposal. "And an Ambassador with those outside the Court could be useful—"

One of them—he suspected Willow—whispered quickly, "Already doing a damn sight better than Matron at playing ..." and Heather shushed her, mouthing what was likely an apology in face of a sharp look from Rosalyn. Andrew winced in anticipation but didn't bother entertaining the notion that his reaction had gone unnoticed; upon glancing at the rest of the Court, he saw Sophie looking at him in what he hoped was approval. Her eyes were more pits of shadow than anything else. As if making eye contact had prompted her, the quiet girl spoke up.

"Mr Endley knows the rules enough to understand consequences. If he wishes to play, I say we let him."

"Agreed. He can play, as long as he stays in line. An adult can't be part of the Court, but he can be an Ambassador." Rosalyn's proclamation was met with nods from the three other visible Court members.

Andrew sighed in relief; he would have to be just as careful as he had been, but this would hopefully allow him to interact with them with reduced risk to him. Of a sort, anyway—he now had to worry about overstepping his boundary as 'Ambassador', rather than their wrath at his very presence.

They were looking at him expectantly—he cleared his throat and spoke quickly. "Thank you, Queen Rosalyn."

He almost felt like he should say something more, but he didn't know what, exactly.

Should he leave, now? Andrew shifted his weight, about to take a step towards the doorway, but one of the girls spoke suddenly, stopping him mid-motion. "We should have a ballroom! Like a *proper* castle!"

Andrew felt himself gape in disbelief for a moment, and quickly closed his mouth. He could sort of understand the demand—if the house was being rebuilt, the idea of just adding an extra room or making their castle 'better' probably seemed reasonable to a child—but agreeing to that simply wasn't an option. Convincing them to forget the notion was urgent, before the rest of the spirits agreed, and he went to speak, to throw together a sound reasoning that they would accept, but Rosalyn got there first.

"And where would we put it, Princess Marie? In the garden? It would block the path and cover the tree."

The hawthorn tree in question had been mostly destroyed by the fire—only about a metre or two of jagged stump remained—but Andrew knew better than to mention that. Perhaps to the spirits, the tree still reached high?

"I meant inside ... Like in Matron's study, no one uses that anymore."

"If I may," Andrew chose then to interject; Rosalyn's expression had turned considering, rather than irritated, "the addition of a ballroom would make it impossible to restore the rest of the castle to its former glory."

The Clover Court turned as one to stare at him, and the reminder that his safety wasn't guaranteed slammed into him like a sledgehammer. "If—" He cleared his voice to try to stop it from shaking. "I think," he began again, mind racing to improvise something convincing, "that a ballroom would be better suited to the attic; that way, it would span the entire castle and could serve as a good home for the throne. After all, balls wouldn't be held year-round, surely, and having it in the throne-room would stop non-Royals from entering unwanted."

Silence, as the ghosts considered his idea.

He took a deep breath.

They hadn't turned down the proposal yet, but Andrew knew that if they did still want a ballroom made in the main floors of the house, he would be forced to disappoint them. He dearly hoped it wouldn't come to that.

The setting sun had darkened the room considerably, but Andrew didn't dare light his torch. The ghosts gave no light, and he found himself relying on the hints of their appearances that he could still see.

Ash began to drift from the ceiling.

"Fine. The Throne Room can also be the ballroom." Andrew sighed in relief as Rosalyn spoke, his stomach starting to unclench from the ball it had knotted into as soon as Marie had demanded an extra room.

With that, the visible Court members vanished, almost seeming to be swallowed by the gloom, with the exception of Rosalyn. Still sitting on the workbench, she leaned back a little; Andrew assumed that she was resting her hand on it.

"Goodbye for now, Ambassador. The meeting is over."

Andrew took a step forward, raising his hand—he wanted to talk to her without the others there—but she too was gone. Andrew was left in the silent, deserted manor, with only the dust and work tools to watch him sigh, and shudder, and hurry from the darkened building on shaking legs.

Chapter Three – Murmurings and Malice

(January 1940)

Over time, he fitted the pieces of their game into a macabre puzzle, aided by the occasional running footsteps and whispers and drawings done in crayon. Half of the jigsaw had been completed by Rosalyn; he still didn't know if she'd intended to show him as much as she had. From the catapult of memories, he knew they viewed adults with disdain, and so he decided to keep interactions with them as minimal as he could. He played along with their game whenever he found himself at the house, alone aside from the ghosts, pretending to be an Ambassador from the village kingdom to their 'Royal Clover Court'. He pretended not to notice them following him when he spoke to the builders, and he never commented to them how sometimes, as he picked up his bicycle and cycled out through the front gate, he'd feel or glimpse one of them trying to follow him. He wasn't even sure that it was Rosalyn every time.

The existence of the spirits of the two youngest children was only confirmed once all of the walls had been completed and the stairs put in. This time, the wooden staircase was reinforced with metal, for both his own peace of mind and the ghosts. He'd been avoiding the Clover Court—an argument had erupted in the dormitory moments after he'd excused himself, and Rosalyn had brought out that accursed hammer. Leaving as quickly as he could without drawing their ire, Andrew had speed-walked down the corridor and turned left towards the stairs, only to stop short.

A metal bucket, old, dented, and blackened by soot, sat at the top of the stairs. He was being watched. The Court were still arguing; their voices audible like a skipping record, the words incomplete to him but undoubtedly angry. He glanced back, suddenly worried about the hammer swinging at him, but nothing seemed to have changed. The corridor was empty. The landing was empty aside from the bucket. He was still being watched. He tried to ignore how his heart was starting to pound in his chest. This wasn't someone he knew, even distantly, like Heather. Hesitantly, he started to speak. "Hello? Is someone here? I'm sorry for disturbing—"

He took a step forward as he spoke, and the moment he did, the bucket jerked, as though pushed, and crashed down the new stairs, leading him to flinch at the racket. It landed on the ground floor with a clatter and rocked back and forth on its side. Stunned, he stared at it, following the blackened rim with his eyes as it teetered to and fro.

The snatches of hissed words and furious jabs coming from the dormitory had stopped. The Clover Court had heard it too. Outside, it began to rain, heavy enough for the deluge of water to bounce off the windows, as if it were hail. The noise of the bucket rolling back and forth on the hardwood floor gradually petered out as the bucket finally came to a stop. The new-to-him spirit was still there. He couldn't see them, but that feeling of being watched hadn't faded.

"Ugh, go *away*, Olivia!" Marie's voice rang out from the direction of the dormitory, jarringly loud. "Go play with Susan, idiot, 'stead of breaking the castle!"

The 'new' spirit, the piecemeal remains of Olivia—he faintly recalled a little girl, barely more than a toddler, playing hopscotch indoors, lying face down on a smoking floor—was gone a moment later.

As soon as he made it back to his residence, he recounted the interaction in his notes and added both 'Olivia' and 'Susan' to the list of spirits residing at Hawthorne House. It was with some relief that he recorded the two of them as *'residual spirits'*, rather than the full corporeal apparitions of the older girls; hopefully they were more at rest than the Court were, with their unfortunate circumstances.

At least at first, he never touched an item that stood out starkly from the whirlwind of spiders and crayons and fire that made up Rosalyn's memories, even though they all appeared to him over the months it took to rebuild. Andrew had thought to expect them: the hammer with nails, the silver locket, the enamelled brooch, the jar of bugs.

He pretended not to see the canning jar two-thirds full with dead butterflies and beetles when it fell over on a bookshelf, having not been there when he'd entered the barely furnished library. Rosalyn had tolerated his touching the crown, but he doubted Sophie's forgiveness extended far enough to spare him her anger. The enamelled brooch only appeared to him once, whilst he was helping pass tools to a carpenter—word had spread of Andrew's intention to rebuild Hawthorne House, not helped by his renting a room in the town, and finding craftsmen to hire was becoming difficult. He hesitated, but then found himself reaching for the brooch despite his misgivings; he was sure the brooch belonged to Heather, who was either avoiding him or just manifested very little. He wanted to find out more about her. The carpenter said something and he glanced away, distracted, and when he looked back, it was gone.

He ignored Willow's locket when he first spotted it amongst the copper piping set out by the plumber, but when it didn't vanish, he began to consider. Willow had only shown neutrality to him, especially once he'd apologised for startling her at their first meeting, and although he knew she was possessive of the locket, she would surely have hidden it from him if she didn't want him examining it. Besides, he would appreciate the chance to understand past events from her perspective, especially so given her arrival at the orphanage after the game's start. His fingertips brushed the silver facing, a previously unnoticed callus caught on the rim, and he recoiled as his mouth filled with what sewage must taste like, the stench trapped in his nostrils, choking his throat. It was all he could do to turn away and grab for the closest bucket, racing against his accelerating nausea before he vomited.

The locket was gone by the time he'd recovered. The next time he attempted to touch Willow's locket, nothing happened beyond a sense of deep discomfort that took a worryingly long time to fade. He rarely saw the locket again, and Willow even less, only a glimpse of her plaits and shoes as she turned a corner or left a room.

❋ ❋ ❋

By August 1940, the manor was mostly completed, with only superficial additions needed: curtains, books for the library, crockery, linens and such for the beds. The rebuilt and refurbished Hawthorne House was to be kept in reserve for evacuees, even though the local families were already talking about not allowing their children, no matter their origin, up to the House. Although Andrew made a point of extending hospitality, as the manager, he privately agreed with the townspeople; the Clover Court might not react well to living children staying there for extended periods of time. If evacuees were to stay at Hawthorne House, it wouldn't be a matter of 'if' the Court would get involved with their lives, but a matter of 'when'—Andrew felt a sick, heavy weight drop into his stomach as he considered how the Court might respond to living children in their castle. And if one member of the Court took an interest, the others would be sure to involve themselves as well. Ideally, any evacuees would never learn of the ghosts that also inhabited the building, but Andrew had seen how the Clover Court played; if the living children did not want to play with them or pretended that they weren't there, the Court would *force* them to take part in their awful game. And given how far their game had escalated in the weeks before the fire that Rosalyn had instigated, the last thing Andrew wanted was more dead children.

He'd scheduled a meeting with the local council in order to talk matters out once the manor was fully furnished, but for now, he busied himself with walking through the entire place, noting down anything unfinished or missing, having to step over the occasional chalk drawing or mess of thumbtacks on the floor.

He wasn't sure if such things were meant for him, but he erred on the side of caution and didn't engage with it; as soon as he entered the dormitory that had originally belonged to the Clover Court, the now familiar sensation of being closely observed bore into him. Nothing was obviously amiss in the room, and so he glanced around before offering a quick apology for interrupting, and promptly left.

On his way towards the stairs that led up to the next floor, a rhythmic thumping noise caught his attention. He paused, but that feeling of being watched remained—the repetitive thudding wasn't from whoever was following him, this was someone else. He couldn't help the shiver that ran across his skin; he'd *never* get used to that sensation.

Andrew took a moment to compose himself, then stepped around the corner, expecting to see Marie, for he strongly suspected it was Sophie at his back. Rosalyn would have said something by now, and he didn't think the Phillips sisters were the types to shadow someone. It wasn't Marie at the foot of the narrow stairs up to the attic, swinging that awful hammer over and over and over again at something on the floor.

It was Rosalyn. She was bringing the hammer down again and again onto a mess of webbing and black specks— tiny spiders were fleeing to the sides and up the stairs, thousands of them—and though the girl was translucent, the hammer seemed worryingly solid. It certainly sounded like it was, and each impact vibrated through the soles of his shoes. The longer he stared, the less the broken nest looked like spider silk: one moment, the hammer came down on tangled webs, the next, onto a pile of fleshy maggots, then onto full-grown spiders, coated in white ash.

He looked up, following the swing of the hammer, and Rosalyn's crown slipped a little on her head, lopsided and flickering. Andrew opened his mouth, then closed it again, wanting to offer something to comfort her, to rid her of the pure fury that drove the hammer, the way her shoulders shook with upset, with *grief*. But what could he say? Something was wrong, and Andrew was missing the piece of the puzzle that would let him figure it out without asking her. That would be cruelly intrusive, to question her and then be unable to help without disrupting the delicate balancing act that he performed every time he visited

Hawthorne House. After all, to the girls, he was playing their game, and interfering too much would probably be held against him.

The tap of a shoe behind him, and he looked back, knowing as he did that not attempting to comfort Rosalyn was the right choice to make: Sophie was standing a few metres away, and the crown was fully formed on her head, without the flickering of Rosalyn's. One hand held the canning jar, a spindle-legged spider crawling out from her sleeve and dropping onto the curved glass, and she was lifting her free hand to hide the start of a small, satisfied smile.

Sophie was the Queen again, which explained why Rosalyn was so furiously upset. What had Sophie done to usurp her? He wanted to find out, but he found Sophie much harder to read than Rosalyn, likely because it had been Rosalyn who had held the Queenship when he'd picked up the crown, Rosalyn who had shown her memories to him. For a moment, he contemplated asking Sophie to let him touch the crown again—doing so might show him what could possibly outdo the fire to let her win over Rosalyn—but before he could begin to open his mouth, she had disappeared. He could still feel her stare, though, and Rosalyn hadn't reacted to him being there, and so he left her to it, resolving to apologise later for accidentally leading Sophie to witness her anger.

Sophie continued to follow him until he reached the front gates of the grounds. She didn't show herself again or say anything, but as he kept having to brush dead moths and crumpled butterfly wings off his shoulders and empty his pockets of spiders, he was sure the new Queen was still present.

At the completion of Hawthorne House to both his standards and theirs, he requested another meeting with the Clover Court. Sophie had kept her title, although he didn't know how long it would last, and this time, all five of them allowed him to see them, even if they mostly ignored him once he'd said his piece. Andrew had called the meeting to propose both the idea of hosting evacuees for the war effort and of running tours in the manor once the war was over; the revenue would allow for the continued upkeep of Hawthorne House and prevent it from becoming derelict.

Already the informal caretaker of the House and the land it was situated on, Andrew offered to become the official caretaker in addition to his being the manager, allowing him to regularly visit without having to hire someone else to look after the House, to which they unanimously agreed. One of the girls, he thought it was Willow, said something about how they wouldn't want a new adult showing up; Andrew knew the rules, a new caretaker wouldn't listen to them. Andrew had to agree with that assessment, and with that, they considered the matter closed before he had the chance to ask their opinion on living children staying in the house. Queen Sophie dismissed him, and when he didn't immediately walk away, the children vanished at Sophie's example; he heard something fall in the attic and assumed that they continued the meeting there.

※ ※ ※

The evacuees didn't stay in the house for more than a year, despite the ample rooms. Andrew had seen it coming and had done what he could to avoid what he feared happening; the Clover Court forcing the city children to play their game. It had taken longer than he had expected, to be fair; fuelled by a healthy fear of ghosts and Andrew repeatedly warning them not to talk to the spirits, the evacuees had managed to avoid being tangled up with the Clover Court for several months. He counted himself lucky to have caught it when he did—on one visit to the house to try to convince the Court yet again not to play with them, no matter how annoying they were in their accidental disrespect, he'd found one of the evacuees crying, trying to untangle barbed wire from around his ankle and shoe. He'd calmed the little boy down and fetched a pair of wire cutters; upon cutting away all the barbed wire, he'd told him not to play with the see-through girls anymore. Even though they were pushy. The Clover Court denied responsibility, but Andrew was certain they were lying to him. He wasn't sure which Princess had been the one to try to include Thomas-from-London, but he refused to let this continue.

It took a week longer than he was comfortable with—unlike those in charge of the evacuees, Andrew understood how far the Court could escalate their game in a week—as well as testimonies from all ten of the children staying in Hawthorne House, but eventually, they were all found places to live in the town. Predictably, the rumours and dares to sneak into the grounds increased after that, and Andrew had to both lock the gates and have a fence installed at the back of the house to prevent people from climbing over the wall into the garden.

His notes on their manifestations expanded greatly. He kept track of who wore the crown, as it didn't remain in Sophie's hands. Eventually, he moved into Hawthorne House, living as far from the Court's dormitory as he could. He wasn't as disheartened as he probably should have been when the townspeople began avoiding him, calling him 'obsessed'.

Chapter Four – Received in Rote

(February 1950)

Rosalyn stared out of the window at the cloudy skies above, hanging low with their hefty baggage of rain. She didn't think it would pour just yet, but that time was surely drawing closer and closer. Her feet swung back and forth, the toes of her shoes inches above Sophie's pillow. If she stopped focusing on the clouds, she began to see the tracks of raindrops on the glass in front of her face—

She hastily tore her mind away from that train of thought. It wasn't raining, even though it was winter again. It was nearly always winter. It was nearly always raining; such were the whims of England.

A low rumbling noise caught her attention, and she leaned forwards a little, resting her hand on the windowsill to brace herself. There, coming around the bend of the hill; a vehicle that she recognised as a car, even though it looked very different to what she was used to seeing. Mr Endley had shown them pictures of what cars looked like now, after seeing one had caused some upset. It trundled down the road and vanished from sight, probably heading to the main driveway and the front gate. Visitors, most likely.

Were the Court expecting new arrivals? It took her a few minutes to mull it over, but she did remember Marie telling them all that Mr. Endley had said something about more people visiting. Rosalyn supposed this must be them, then. It didn't feel like two weeks had passed since that meeting, but it was hard enough to keep track of their Court rankings, let alone how much time had slid by. Without Matron there to enforce bedtime and meals, the days and weeks and months and years tended to blend together. Especially so since their castle had been rebuilt. Mr Endley was a constant, though, and the Court knew that he would inevitably join them; the House was just as attached to him as it was to them, but at least he was kinder to them than Matron had ever been.

The low rumble of the car stopped, and Rosalyn pushed herself off the windowsill as she heard the distant slam of the car doors and the nervous murmuring of voices. New dignitaries visiting was always an exciting time for the Clover Court, and so Rosalyn ran from the dormitory to the main staircase to witness their arrival at the castle.

Marie was already standing on the landing when Rosalyn arrived, but she didn't do anything except give Rosalyn a warning look. A bucket was teetering precariously on the railing in front of Marie; Rosalyn went past to take a seat on the top stair and saw Willow sitting directly below in the entrance hall, a book open in her lap.

A key clicked in the front door and Rosalyn turned her head to watch as it creaked open, and from the corner of her eye she saw the bucket fall, only to land with a crash on empty, dusty floorboards; Willow had vanished to join Heather in the garden before it had landed. Rosalyn didn't bother to hide the giggle that spilled out of her, letting out a proper laugh as Marie rolled her eyes and stormed off in a huff at her plan being spoiled. Nice try, Princess, but you *missed*.

Mr Endley's voice drifted up from the front door, and Rosalyn refocused on the visitors, who were busily crowding in behind him and looking around curiously at the interior of Hawthorne House. They were all grown-ups, and some of them were pointing at the bucket that Marie had tried to hit Willow with. Rosalyn hastily covered her mouth with her hand to hide her laughter—it was most rude of her to greet foreign Ambassadors in such a manner—and straightened her back to regard the adults carefully.

Sometimes, visitors came back, and so she looked for any familiar faces. After all, Mr Endley had started off as just a visitor, but then he'd picked up her crown, and now he was just as tied to the House as the Clover Court were. He'd be joining them at some point, but she wasn't in a hurry to speed up his permanent arrival: if she did, he might be upset with them, and end up even worse to them than Matron had been. Some of the visitors were carrying papers and clipboards, and quite a few had strange-looking metal objects in their hands, each one slender and bent at a right-angle. How odd.

With Heather and Willow in the garden and Marie in the dormitory, Rosalyn concentrated for a moment to locate Sophie; the Queen had been in their attic Throne Room before the guests had arrived, but she wasn't there now. Sophie was—

Sophie was very close by. Not seeing any sign of her on the stairs or in the front hall, Rosalyn twisted around to look back at the first-floor landing. The air wavered and as Rosalyn watched, Sophie appeared there, standing close to the bannister. She was wearing the crown, but not carrying the Royal Sceptre; it wasn't needed at the moment. A spider crawled up from the underside of the landing, the eight spindly legs hauling it over the edge and carrying it up the closest wooden spoke, climbing towards the top of the bannister. Sophie floated forwards to cup her hands around it, not bothering to walk, and both she and Rosalyn looked down at the adult visitors. She decided against mentioning how the distinction between mud-beetles and butterflies didn't even matter now; the Queen wasn't currently against her, so she would save it until she had a reason to needle Sophie.

There were eyes on them, so Rosalyn returned to looking down the grand staircase to see one of the visitors, a lady in a dark peacoat, staring back at her, mouth agape. She looked somewhat familiar—she must have visited before. Rosalyn quickly placed a finger to her lips.

Shhh.

She felt Sophie lean forwards to examine the newcomers, and both girls knew that the Queen had made herself invisible to all but the Clover Court. The lady's mouth closed, but she started elbowing the person next to her rather frantically.

Ash began to drift down from the landing and dust the floorboards underneath in the hall, interspersed with the occasional butterfly or moth wing—a result of their combined, sustained waiting there.

Down on the ground floor, the bucket shifted slowly to one side, dragging over Willow's book until the rim hit the floorboard; Rosalyn stood up and leaned against the bannister to get a better look. The visitors pointed and murmured amongst themselves; from her vantage point, Rosalyn watched Willow flip the book shut, ignoring the crumpled pages—Rosalyn assumed that the Princess would smooth them out once she had safely hidden it somewhere. One of the visitors, a tall man with combed-back hair, muttered something about the bucket and the book moving on their own. Willow looked up at the landing, correctly assuming that a Princess would still be there; Rosalyn shrugged at her puzzled expression, then nodded meaningfully at the perturbed crowd. Clearly, the visitors couldn't see Princess Willow, a fact that she finally realised.

If *she'd* been the one down there, Rosalyn would have let them see her, just for a moment, but Willow didn't seem to grant the dignitaries the same treatment that her betters would—instead of showing herself, the younger Princess merely picked up her book and tucked it under her arm, before rolling her eyes and vanishing. Predictably, she'd taken the book with her, but not the bucket ... hmm. *She left a mess. Maybe I should have a talk with her about respect for the castle.* Mr Endley had worked so hard on it, after all. There wouldn't be any need to involve the Queen in this, but Rosalyn would have to wait until after the visitors had left.

One of the visitors called out, his voice wavering a little, and Rosalyn hastily turned her attention back to them. It wouldn't do to ignore the dignitaries, even unintentionally. "Hello? Are you Princess Rosalyn?"

Tilting her head at both his audacity and at how unsure he sounded, Rosalyn took note of where the rest of the Court were. Willow and Heather were still in the garden, Queen Sophie was in the dormitory, and Marie was up in the Throne Room. She drew herself up; as the most senior—and only—Princess present, greeting the dignitaries was her responsibility. "Yes, I am. Welcome to Hawthorne Castle. The Royal Clover Court will receive you shortly."

The visitors took a collective step backwards as she spoke, and Rosalyn frowned—that was *most rude*. The drifting ash fell thicker now, and she began to descend the stairs. She heard the Queen's hum of disapproval, faint but clear—Queen Sophie must have been listening through the open dormitory door—and a weight fell into Rosalyn's hand, her fingers closing around the smooth wooden shaft as it did. The nails in the head of the Sceptre bumped against her ankle, so she hefted it up to hold it with both hands. She hadn't been allowed to wield the Sceptre since she'd last held the Queenship; the weight felt almost wrong, as if she were breaking a rule. But Queen Sophie had placed it in her grip, and so Rosalyn couldn't be held to account for 'misbehaviour'.

The Sceptre was in Rosalyn's hands, and the visitors clearly saw it; the woman who'd first noticed her spoke hurriedly, twisting the metal prong in shaking hands. "I—we apologise for any rudeness—it was unintentional! It's a pleasure to meet you?"

Hm. Rosalyn had expected them to double-down, not recognise their misstep ... She looked to the Queen, invisible to the visitors on the landing, silently asking if they should be forgiven.

Beetle wings joined the falling ash.

The Queen considered it.

The visitors were silent, but Rosalyn paid them no mind. If they stepped out of line, the Queen would know. The Sceptre vanished from Rosalyn's hands—her grip closed around nothing, her nails hitting her palms—and reappeared in the Queen's left hand. She let the head drop to the floor before turning dismissively and walking back towards the dormitory, dragging the Sceptre with her. Rosalyn watched her round the corner, the nail heads scraping on the floorboards, before she looked back down to the visitors. Were they aware of how Rosalyn would have shown the Court's offence?

The Queen had forgiven them for their transgression against a Princess, but they were on thin ice. The Court would be watching for any more missteps.

They seemed to have recovered their pitiful confidence and poise, no longer clustered quite so tightly at the front door. Good. Dignitaries who could not even meet a Princess with grace would not garner any goodwill with the Clover Court, to the visitors' detriment. Princess Rosalyn returned to the top of the stairs, pleased with her relative vantage point, and sat back down to observe the group.

Their activities as the Clover Court were so much more interesting now, with Mr Endley acting as a liaison between the Royal Court and visiting dignitaries. With all these other new kingdoms to consider, the Queen and her Princesses were busier than ever before. Sitting on the steps of their castle, Princess Rosalyn was content with the thought that they would play forever.

Epilogue

Rules for Traversing Hawthorne House and the Walled Garden:

(1951 edition, compiled since the manor's reconstruction and restoration in 1939-40 by Mr. Andrew Endley)

1) Ask permission from the 'Royal Clover Court' before taking any actions.

2) Before entering the grounds, ensure you have written permission dated at least a fortnight (two weeks) in advance.

3) You must be accompanied by a guide familiar with and licensed to enter Hawthorne House at all times.

4) Do not trespass in Hawthorne House.

5) Do not strike a match or light any kind of fire.

6) No photography is allowed.

7) The spirits are generally benevolent, as long as care is taken not to antagonise or provoke them. Do not intentionally do so.

8) Do not disturb any drawings you may find.

9) Do not attempt entry into the Attic.

10) Do not force entry through a locked, obstructed, or otherwise sealed door.

11) Do not disturb the spirits unless they decide to interact with you; they are playing a make-believe game known as 'The Royal Clover Court'. For more information on 'The Royal Clover Court' and the spirits residing in Hawthorne House, see overleaf.

12) Ouija boards are not permitted unless under strict supervision by your guide.

13) Do not make any permanent markings or damage anything; any property damage will be charged to you.

14) If you come across the following items, do not touch or approach any of them. Vacate the room immediately before informing your guide.

- A circle of barbed wire.

- A wooden hammer with nails in the hammerhead.

- A piece of paper with neat penmanship and molten red wax.

- A sealed canning jar (containing either ashes or a multitude of dead, winged insects).

- A silver pendant locket, tarnished and dented.

- An enamelled brooch.

Rules for Interacting with 'The Royal Clover Court':

1) You may ask for details of their game, but do not make suggestions or try to alter the rules; they will become hostile.

2) Be respectful when interacting with the spirits.

3) Do not ask for details regarding the fire.

4) The current 'Queen' is whichever spirit is wearing a 'crown' made from barbed wire; defer to whomever it may be.

   (Note: Rosalyn is the exception to this; she has been seen wearing the 'crown' no matter if another is currently the 'Queen'.)

5) Do not try to tell any of the spirits what to do. This applies doubly to whichever is acting as 'Queen'.

6) If they attempt to include you in their game, play along as little as you are able to. If the Queenship changes whilst you are there, vacate the room and

inform your guide immediately. Pay attention to whom it changed to. This may not be instantly obvious.

Known Spirits and Signs of Their Presence:

1) Marie Moore – A ten-year-old girl who frequently upsets the other spirits, sometimes seen holding a wooden, bloodied hammer. The most likely to become hostile to visitors. She wears a green dress. Signs of her presence include the smell of ash or burning wax, small items such as crayons, pencils, or candles being thrown at visitors, and thumbtacks left in pockets, underfoot, or on chairs.

2) Rosalyn Pearson – The most frequent spirit sighted at Hawthorne House. Aged nine, she wears a purple and white dress, and is often seen with a 'crown' made from barbed wire. The most likely to interact with and be amicable to visitors, but she has a tendency to leave without warning and/or draw the attention of less benevolent spirits. Signs of her presence include the barbed wire 'crown', four-leafed clovers, crayons, and falling ash.

3) Sophie Whittel – A taciturn, watchful girl who tends to observe visitors instead of directly interact. Sophie seems detached compared to Rosalyn or Marie. She does not speak much or show herself often but may do so if asked politely. The canning jar belongs to Sophie; dead winged bugs are a sign of her presence, particularly butterflies, moths, and beetles. Other signs include

spiders (living or dead), an intense feeling of being stared at or through, and the smell of woodsmoke. She is nine years old and wears a dark blue dress. Her hair and eyes are dark.

4) Willow Phillips – An eight-year-old girl who appears infrequently. Willow is skittish and shy; most sightings of her have been momentary—her name is only known due to surviving records. She wears brown or red and her hair is tied in two long plaits. It is speculated that the silver locket belonged to Willow. Finding pieces of chalk or crayons in odd places may be Willow's doing. The younger sister of Heather (see below).

5) Heather Phillips – Willow's elder sister, ten years old. The only spirit with a clear injury; blood constantly drips from a pockmarked line across her forehead. She is fearful of Sophie and Marie and has stated a dislike for Rosalyn. Reluctantly involved in their game; she will become hostile at its mention. A sudden, uncharacteristic onset of claustrophobia is attributed to Heather's presence; if there are other signs, they are not known.

6) Olivia Bailey – A five-year-old girl who appears far less frequently than the above spirits; she has been sighted running up and down the stairs and heard playing in the nursery. Allegedly the cause of an incident in the laundry room where a metal bucket was thrown at a visitor's legs.

7) Susan Parr – A very young girl, assumed to be around four years old. Not much is known about her. According to Rosalyn, she does not appear

often, and when she does, Olivia is with her. She has been heard crying on the first or second floor.

Acknowledgements

To Mum, Dad, and my siblings, for supporting me and hearing my ideas as I worked on the novella.

My friends, who mean the world to me.

Marilyn, whose outings to the bookshop I cherished growing up.

About the Author

Hadassah Shiradski is a dark fiction writer from South-East England. Preferring to write short-form gothic horror, she has a love of atmospheric horror puzzle games, botany, historical fashion, and folklore.

Content Warnings

Intense bullying
Child abuse and endangerment
Child harm
Detailed depictions of child death
Abuse (physical and psychological)
Neglect
Death

MORE FROM BRIGIDS GATE PRESS

A tragic accident, shrouded in mystery, leads to a family reunion in the hidden village of Little Hatchet, located in the smothering shadow of GodBeGone Wood, the home of the mythical Woodcutter and Grandma. Alec Eades rediscovers his bond with GodBeGone Wood and the future his father agreed to years ago as nefarious landowner Oliver Hayward schemes to raise money for the village by re-enacting part of the Woodcutter legend. Old wounds are reopened and ties of blood and friendship are tested to the extreme when the Woodcutter is summoned and Grandma returns.

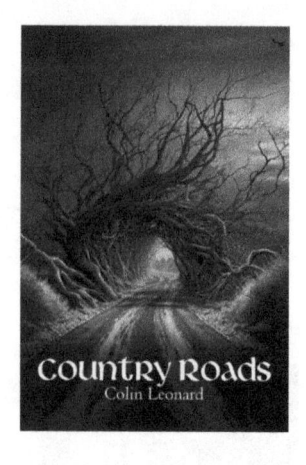

Something is outside; in the fields, by the ditches, on the roads. Something old and cruel and vicious. When Luke Sheridan moves out of Dublin city to rural Kilcross with his wife and baby, he imagines the worst part will be his extended commute to work. They can look forward to enjoying the countryside and being part of a small community. After all, his old friend Declan Maguire lives in the house next door and is a Garda in the nearest town. But Declan's devilish attitude towards drink, drugs and women means trouble is never far from his door. And worse, gruesome murders and the appearance of sinister figures at night mean the countryside is becoming a very dangerous place to live. Country Roads—don't go outside alone.

the patient routine
luna rey hall

Ashton is convinced they are dying. whether it be from cancer, heart disease, or a fungal infection, they know something bad is always about to happen. after a night of health-related panic attacks, & urged by a voice in their head, Ashton decides to check in to the ER again but when another patient is brought in with an unknown ailment that puts the entire hospital on lockdown, Ashton may be trapped in their worst nightmare.

According to Dante, a sin is the misdirection of love-the human will, or essentially, the direction of our beings. Love the Sinner is an examination of just how those sins can kaleidoscope into horrific consequences creating a distorted and deadly landscape. These stories stand stark before you in full glaring misstep and macabre to show the human psyche in all its twisted reality. From grief and its rage to medical meddling to ensure a new world order to bloody revenge within a quantum leap, these stories seek to solidify one absolute truth: man is the scariest monster.

Visit our website at: www.brigidsgatepress.com